FORTUNA'S QUEEN

Forgotten Women of History Book 2

ANNE R BAILEY

Inkblot Press

Dedicated to the family and friends who have supported me in this endeavor.

PROLOGUE

Pella, 356 BC

She was the daughter of the king of Epirus.

Yet here she was on her knees before Phillip of Macedonia, her husband.

She was rumored to have descended from the great Achilles himself, and if the rumors were accurate she had enough magic in her thumb to squash an empire. She wished that were true.

"Don't go." Her voice barely a whisper.

She kept her eyes to the ground as he stepped off his dais and approached her. She couldn't help but stiffen when he touched her bare shoulder with his hand.

"We all must do what is necessary for the kingdom." He lifted her off the ground and placed a kiss on her cold lips. "My beautiful wife, you must stay here and guard the kingdom and yourself." He placed a hand over her protruding belly.

"Take me with you then." She did not relent, even as she saw his eyes narrow in frustration and anger.

She was not some complacent cow to be left at home.

"Olympias." He chided her like her father used to when she was a little girl. "You should go rest."

She pulled out of his arms and stormed out of the hall in a flourish of gold and white linen.

The courtiers parted to let her through. They watched as this untouchable lady who commanded their respect brushed away the servants who moved forward to help her. Damn her husband, she cursed in her head as she marched down the halls and corridors.

It was only in her rooms among her loyal servants and her pets that her icy mask cracked and her fury reared its head.

She flung a vial of perfume, smiling satisfied when it hit the opposite wall and shattered, filling the air with the sweet smell of narcissus.

"Leave it," she hissed at a servant who bent to clean up the shards. "Leave, all of you." She dismissed her servants with a wave of her hand.

Olympias was well known for her fits of anger, and they left without another word. Ever since she had become pregnant these fits had increased in frequency. All the astrologers predicted that she was carrying a great warrior in her belly.

Olympias sat down on her couch piled high with silk cushions as she tried to calm herself.

The baby was kicking now.

"Warrior, indeed," she murmured as she caressed her belly, urging the child to calm down.

Phillip seemed determined to leave her behind as he went off to conquer new lands and expand his kingdom. She knew it was likely that she would be usurped from her position as his principal wife while he was away. Lords and kings alike would push forward their daughters, sisters, and nieces, hoping to catch the lustful king's eye. However, this was not the greatest danger she had sensed. She feared there would be a rift between father and son that could never be mended.

So bending the knee, she hoped she might prevail upon him to put off his campaigning for another month—no more. It was foolish to ask this, but for her son she would do anything. She would see him come to his throne, but for the moment his future was clouded and Olympias was scared what this meant.

She was also filled with anxiety that while Phillip was away from her Attalus would whisper in his ear until he finally convinced her husband she was a witch and that her son was not worthy to be his heir.

Phillip had another son by one of his inconsequential wives, but the child was slow and Phillip was eager to have a healthy replacement. It had been rumored that the child who had been born to a great destiny had been cursed by his nursemaid, who had been caught weaving a magical spell over him on the night of his first birthday.

One thing Phillip feared more than dying of old age was magic.

Olympias rolled her eyes at his fears and pitied the nursemaid, who had died a terrible death for doing nothing more than singing to her young charge a lullaby in her native tongue.

Such simple actions could be misinterpreted so easily,

and the courtiers who were always searching for scandal had pounced on the opportunity to make trouble.

That had been nearly two years ago, when Olympias had arrived at the palace a fresh-faced youth. She had learned quickly to guard her secrets and do what she had to do to gain power in her own right.

As Phillip's wife, there was always a crowd of men and women dogging her steps, asking her to intercede with her husband on their behalf. Over the years, she had gained a loyal following and they protected her from the likes of Attalus. He was one of Phillip's most trusted commanders, who had high ambitions of connecting himself to the Argead dynasty through marriage. Attalus had plenty of pretty nieces, and Phillip's eyes were always wandering.

Luckily, Attalus was busy now with thoughts of war, but he was sure to return to his scheming the minute the fighting stopped. She frowned, wishing the gods would take his life in battle so she could be rid of him, but she had already scried his future and saw that death was not imminent for her rival.

She had to content herself with the fact that she would remain in Pella as Phillip's representative watching over his house. She would be alone to create further alliances and gain more power while both men were away.

Still, it was with a heavy heart that she watched Phillip depart at the head of his army.

He was a warrior through and through. He was not like other commanders who hung back while their soldiers fought their battles for them. This was the one thing she admired about him.

She watched him now standing in front of the altar holding the large sacrificial dagger near the bull's head as the priest finished intoning the last of the prayer to Ares to bring victory to the Macedonian army.

Olympias felt her heart soar with anticipation as she watched his strong arms swing upward, slicing through the bull's throat as though it was merely butter. She was mesmerized by the blood spurting from the wound as the bull bellowed one last time. It coated the steps of the temple even as the acolytes ran forward with a golden bowl to collect the draining blood.

"Victory!" the head priest called out after consulting the bowl, and a great cheer came from the gathered crowd and soldiers.

This was not to be the last of the sacrifices, but it was the most important. Hundreds of beasts were offered up to the gods to provide a speedy victory.

Phillip was confident that the Pheraeans and Phocians would be defeated swiftly, but he also prayed for a battle worthy of being remembered. He dreamed of glory as all men did and thought of expanding his kingdom. The Thessalian League had approached him last year asking for his help to get rid of the dictator Lycophran, who had managed to anger most of the ancient noble families of Thessaly. They wished to return to the old ways when they could manage their own affairs.

Phillip had jumped at the chance to involve himself in the politics of the region. He secretly dreamed of uniting all the Greek city-states under his name. He would rule all of Greece and then he would turn his attention to his dangerous neighbor to the east. The Persians were a constant threat and he dreamed of one day conquering them, but Macedonia could not do it alone.

🝜

Perae, 355 BC

War had dragged on for longer than he had hoped.

He had been on campaign for over two years, and they were finally making steady progress. Ever since the Pheraeans had sacked the Temple of Delphi, his army had been invigorated with a new cause. Now they fought to overthrow the sacrilegious Pheraeans and defend Apollo's honor.

At his side, Nicesipolis stirred, murmuring something in her sleep. Phillip frowned and wrapped his arms around his newest wife to protect her from her evil dreams. In his embrace, she stilled once more and he kissed her brow.

Back in Pella, his newest son Alexander was getting stronger with each passing day. He had been born with a crown of blond hair like his mother's. The child had too much of Olympias in him, and he found himself already resenting the growing boy.

Phillip believed that he was jealous of the love Olympias gave to Alexander. He wanted her to feel the same toward him. In their first years of marriage, he had doted on her and came to love her with a fervor that terrified him at times.

He even put up with the snakes Olympias insisted on keeping, despite the rumors of witchcraft that his courtiers liked to whisper in his ears knowing how terrified he was of evil magic. Desiring her love and admiration, he ignored them, but still he did not receive what he wanted from her.

Instead, she seemed content to threaten him with the gods' wrath if he displeased her.

He worshiped the gods but also trembled at their power.

They had razed cities like Troy to the ground and snuffed the light out of greater men than him.

He had come to his throne by right and ruled with a sword in his hand. He had molded Macedonia from a backwater province into the great kingdom it was today. But in a moment, all of his work could be washed away on the whim of an immortal who cared nothing for the blood and sweat he had poured into his land.

So Phillip harbored a fear of them that he could not get rid of. People liked to claim that he was blessed by the gods, but Phillip would rather he remain anonymous. It was safer than drawing their attention.

Nicesipolis shifted and her hand rested on his chest as though she wanted to comfort and wash away his dark thoughts. It was she who had suggested mildly that he was Apollo's champion.

On his behalf, he should destroy those who had sacked his temple. If he did this, Apollo would see his enemies driven into the sea.

His normally gentle wife had surprised him with her vicious sentiments. Just as soon as she had finished speaking, her usually innocent countenance had returned.

He wondered if she had been touched by a divine vision or influenced by Apollo himself.

The thought had led him to seriously consider his next actions. After conferring with his commanders, he had come up with the perfect plan. His men would go out to battle wearing crowns of laurels for Apollo—they would be his soldiers.

Perhaps Apollo would grant them the victory for the honor they bestowed on him.

It was also a shrewd political move. The Pheraeans and their allies would think twice about continuing to fight against him. Their morale would surely be lost in the face of the righteous wrath of the Macedonian army.

But now his thoughts turned away from war as he regarded his dark-haired Thessalian wife.

She was everything Olympias was not. She might not have been as nobly born, but where Olympias was sharp, she was soft. Where Olympias was war, she was peace.

Phillip ran his hands through Nicesipolis's dark curls. She was an innocent youth, seemingly untouched by ambition or hatred. She loved him with those dark eyes of hers and seemed to melt in his arms.

For his part, he adored her devotion to him. His courtiers and politicians had been surprised when he had declared he would marry her.

They thought perhaps she would be another of his concubines, but he had honored her with a proper marriage. Any children she had would be legitimate heirs. This thought pleased him.

He thought of Alexander again. The last time he had seen him he had kicked at his father and regarded him with a cool hatred when Phillip pulled his mother away to his rooms. Such anger did not belong on a child's face. Did Olympias plot against him and poison his son's mind against him? She was about to give birth again, and he feared that it would be another son, another rival for his throne.

Any children he had with Nicesipolis would surely adore and honor him. Before he allowed himself to fall into a deep sleep, he made a note to call the astrologer tomorrow to read her charts, and after that he would put his soldiers through their paces.

Pella, 349 BC

Olympias drummed her nails on the table, irritated as she listened to the latest report from Thessaly.

The steward looked as though he was about to start quaking in his sandals.

Coiled around her left arm and resting contently on her shoulder blades was her black python, Kelainos. No doubt the steward thought she would have him fed to the snake if he displeased her.

Dressed in a robe as dark as her pet, with her hair piled high on her head and captured in a net of pearls, she looked every bit the sorceress. They were ridiculous, the rumors that sprang forth about her, but she used them to her advantage. Fear gave her control.

"Lydus, are you keeping something from me?" She petted the snake's head with her free hand.

"N-no. That is to say, the king has ordered jewels and silk to be sent to Thessaly. Nothing to trouble yourself over." He bowed low in an effort to hide his shaking.

"There's no need to be afraid. You have been a loyal servant, Lydus. Besides, Kelainos does not bite unless I ask him to." Olympias gave a chilling laugh and dismissed the frightened man. She wondered if he would have fainted if she had tormented him a moment longer.

Once he was gone she snapped her fingers and her personal handmaidens stepped forward. Carefully, they helped her unwind her stubborn pet from her arm and put him back in his basket.

Her favored lady, Niobe, hung by her side waiting for instructions.

"Send him a small purse of silver for his honesty. I fear I may have gone too far with my antics tonight. After that please tell the cooks to be generous with the food and to bring out as much wine as my guests require tonight."

Niobe bowed her head and left to see to her tasks.

Now that she was left alone and without her snake draped over her, Olympias no longer looked like the powerful sorceress queen. She was merely a tired twenty-year-old woman, with two children to look after. She walked to their rooms and watched from afar as they played in the arms of servants.

Alexander was nearly three years old, big for his age, with curly hair like her own. Cleopatra was only two months old and, much to Olympias's dismay, seemed to favor her father's darker appearance, but she was a sweet quiet baby. There was a distinct difference between Cleopatra and Alexander, who even as a newborn had not given his nursemaid a moment's peace.

Lanike, Alexander's nursemaid, spotted her and when he was distracted with a toy walked over to her, bowing respectfully. "The children seem happy today. Cleopatra has just awoken from a nap if you would like to hold her."

Olympias shook her head. She did not have time to play with her children now, but tonight she would pull them into her arms and cradle them until they fell asleep. "Has Alexander been behaving?"

"He tried to escape from us twice, but I caught him."

"He will become unmanageable the more he grows." Olympias shook her head and then left the children to their games.

She was a fiercely protective mother. All the servants had been handpicked and interviewed by her personally. She kept the children close to her own rooms and guarded them against sickness and disease. Phillip wrote to her frequently warning her not to coddle their son. He needed to become a warrior, not a whimpering child hiding behind his mother's skirts.

Olympias was furious he would dare make such an accusation. She dreamed of great things for her golden-haired son, but for now he was too young to protect himself.

Back in her private rooms, her desk was now neatly organized. Scrolls and tablets were neatly arranged for her perusal. There was nothing there that she did not already know. The army needed a constant stream of food and supplies, which she oversaw with an easy proficiency. The rest were the requests of noblemen begging for favors, which could wait a few more days.

She fiddled with the gold band around her left arm. Was Nicesipolis a rival or a passing fancy? She had heard of Phillip's new marriage a few days after it had taken place. He had wanted to keep it quiet, no doubt fearing what she would think, but Olympias had merely shrugged. Phillip had never been faithful, nor did she expect him to be. He was a king and needed to gain favor and power through marriages and alliances.

But then rumors began that this woman who had barely any noble blood in her at all was constantly by his side. At night, she would whisper to him and they would retire before Phillip had too much to drink and became rowdy. Whatever she wanted, he seemed more than happy to procure for her.

"Witchcraft" was whispered among the courtiers and servants at Pella. They had never seen this girl before, but they did not doubt that something was afoot.

Some approached Olympias warning her of this new wife and her magical powers.

"She controls the minds of men with the mere sound of her voice. With a touch, she could send a man to his grave," they whispered.

Olympias laughed and waved them aside. These were the same rumors she had heard about herself. In the past, Phillip had liked to taunt her with them. "My little witch," he had whispered into her silvery blond hair as he clutched her at night.

Then, out of resentment, she began to emulate the very thing he teased her with, and then he began to fear her as well.

To many she had indeed become a witch, but it was not through magic but rather deceit and wit that Olympias kept her enemies at bay. She played one faction against the other until she achieved the outcome she wished for and no one was the wiser. To her friends she was a generous benefactress, to her enemies she was a viper, but she always had to watch her back.

Phillip had begun to keep his distance as well. He did not believe she was a witch, but he was smart enough to know that she had just as deadly skills up her sleeves.

Between her snakes and poisons, he could not trust her, and now that she had a son who had a claim on his throne he was even more fearful, though he was loath to admit that he was afraid of a woman, much less his own wife.

"How the men would laugh if they saw their great ruler shaking before his wife." She remembered laughing at him when he had stumbled into her room one night drunk. He trembled when he saw her with a snake entangled around her middle.

He had backed away frightened, but at her words had stepped forward and rewarded her with a sharp slap. Still she had laughed, and he fled the room.

That had been the last time he had gone to her rooms in nearly a year.

Olympias sighed. Her bed remained cold, but she would not risk taking a lover. Any whiff of scandal would give Phillip the excuse to declare Alexander illegitimate and get rid of her too.

Now Phillip wanted to lavish his favorite with gifts and jewels when the kingdom's coffers were straining from war? Well, who was she to stop him?

※

Thessaly, 348 BC

Phillip held her as she cried into his arms. She had awoken once more from nightmares filled with blood and war.

Ever since the physicians declared she was carrying a child, these bad dreams visited her at night. He hoped this was not an ominous sign from the gods that the child would bring bad luck. His astrologer had read the child's fortune and assured him it was a golden future.

"I see a crown on a dark head and children all around."

Nicesipolis gave a sigh of relief that her child seemed to have such a favorable future. She trusted the astrologers and hung breathless on their every word.

Phillip was not so convinced and asked the astrologers about the dreams.

"Your wife is the kindest of women. She is carrying a child of Ares in her womb, conceived in a time of war and victory. It does not surprise me that she suffers these nightmares. Her humors are out of balance, but it is nothing to fear. A tea will soothe her."

"I will speak with the physician," Nicesipolis promised, grasping Phillip's arm when the baby moved within her. He dismissed the balding old man and sat with her on the soft pillows, running his hands through her hair as he always liked to do.

"You shouldn't worry about me." She did not meet his gaze. "I do not mean to trouble you with my little problems."

He kissed her brow. "You have brought me nothing but good fortune ever since we were married. I like to make sure you are properly looked after."

She giggled at his words and sent him away. He had to meet with his generals shortly, and she did not want him to be late on her account.

Phillip left her under the care of her maids and returned to the world of men. He knew what people whispered behind his back. She had made him soft. He had not even taken another lover when she fell pregnant but chose to stay by her side. Of course, he visited his other wives and paid them the attention they were due. But Nicesipolis was different.

He had great hopes for her children. There had been nothing but victory since he had married her. The Thessalian League had named him archon of Thessaly, he was Apollo's champion, and soon he would have all of Greece under his command. All he wanted now was another heir. He did not trust Alexander. When he looked into his son's eyes he saw his own death looking back at him and hated him for it.

Occasionally, he felt guilty he was not kinder to Alexander, but the anger he felt toward his mother got in the way and he could not bring himself to love Alexander as he should.

Phillip tolerated Olympias for her powerful father, the wealth she had brought as her dowry, and her handling of affairs in Pella. She saw that things ran smoothly even though he had never asked her to help him. Sometimes he wanted to thank her, but then he would meet with her and would find his blood boiling at the sight of her cool gaze. She regarded him as one would look at a wild animal that needed to be tamed, and it made him furious.

He had to find a way to cool his temper besides Nicesipolis's soothing touch.

Weeks passed them by. Wars and battles were being planned and fought. Alliances were being made. But the danger outside the fortified walls did not touch Phillip's new favorite.

Nicesipolis was resting in the inner palace where a sacred grove had been planted.

Her feet dipped in the cooling water that flowed from one end to the other in a steady stream.

Summer was fast approaching and she found herself getting hot despite the fanning of the slaves, though she tried not to complain. It was hard to find time to herself. Phillip's commanders and advisors did not like her. They thought she urged him to pursue peace, not war. In truth, she did nothing more than massage his temples and tend to him as any loving wife did to her weary husband. He was hot-tempered and quick to act rashly if pressed a certain way.

All she tried to do was help him think rationally, but she supposed in the eyes of the court this was evidence of her magic. Where once they could persuade him to make a decision instantly, he now liked to mull it over carefully, planning out what he should do next.

A commotion and footsteps alerted her to trouble. She did not bother rising to her feet. If it was assassins, then at least she would die comfortably.

A tall blond woman appeared, walking up the path in slow sauntering steps.

Was this what the commotion had been about? Nicesipolis raised her eyes to block out the sun.

Ah, yes. She knew who this was. This woman could raise more than a little commotion if she wished. Olympias was rumored to be able to raise hell with the snap of her fingers.

With the help of a slave girl, she rose to her feet. She was seven months along in her pregnancy now, and moving around had become awkward.

Nicesipolis bowed her head low to her superior. "Good afternoon, Lady Olympias. I was not aware you were arriving today or I would have ordered a feast in your honor."

Olympias grinned. "I came to find a sorceress, but instead I find a young pretty woman, heavily pregnant with my husband's child."

"Our husband." Nicesipolis did not miss a beat. Olympias smiled and moved forward to greet her properly with a kiss on the cheek. The slaves around them shifted nervously, wondering if she had some evil plan. They had been instructed to protect Nicesipolis, but would they dare stop Olympias?

"It is wonderful to meet you." Nicesipolis kissed her other cheek. "I've heard so many things about you."

Olympias regarded her with the studious gaze of a scholar. She did not detect sarcasm from her, nor could she sense any maliciousness. When she looked at Nicesipolis's sun-kissed face she saw a kind woman without any secrets.

How peculiar. This was not what she was expecting to find.

Olympias suggested they sit down, and soon the two most powerful women in the Kingdom were dipping their feet in the water as though they were children on the bank of a river.

Phillip's ministers moved out of the way of a slave who hurried in.

"What is it, boy?" Phillip looked up from his papers and recognized one of Nicesipolis's guards.

The boy approached and whispered into his ear that Olympias had appeared unexpectedly. She was with Nicesipolis now in the courtyard.

Phillip frowned. This was rather unexpected news. His gaze shifted to Scylax, his supposed spymaster. Was he in her employ? The man seemed to try to disappear out of the room, but Phillip had more pressing concerns than dealing with Olympias and her followers for now.

He sent the boy away with instructions to keep a close eye on Nicesipolis.

"Bring some water and refreshments please," Nicesipolis called to the servants. She saw them wavering, but her glare sent them running. She was now relatively alone with Olympias. Just outside the courtyard were the guards, but she had no fear of the woman beside her.

"I hope all is well in Pella?" she asked calmly, trying to determine the reason for Olympias's visit.

"Yes. Frankly, I came to see what all the fuss was about." Olympias did not mean to sound so crude, but her counterpart gave her a toothy grin.

"Is it the rumors of my magic? I can assure you I do not have any." She sighed. "I do not have the illustrious birth necessary, but I have seemed to make plenty of enemies."

"Ah. That comes with the territory, but you'll get used to it." Olympias looked at her with a critical eye. No, there was no magic or power here, but there was something about her. She sensed a presence hanging around her. Perhaps she had been favored by the gods, but which one was still unclear.

"Is the child healthy?" Olympias asked, staring at the large belly. She wouldn't be surprised if it was twins.

"They say it will be a boy, but that is only to please Phillip." Nicesipolis saw her flinch. "But I know it is a girl. I think I have seen her in my dreams."

"May I?" She wished to feel her stomach and make a judgment for herself, and Nicesipolis nodded.

As Olympias's cool hand pressed on the stomach, she

felt a powerful kick in response and grinned. There was no flash of future or impending doom from this child. "You have a fighter. Girl or boy, it won't matter. They will be healthy."

Nicesipolis's face was taut with pain. "That is all I can hope for."

The servants reappeared with platters of fruits and pitchers of water, too much for the two ladies to consume, but they enjoyed themselves in the sacred grove until the sun began to set.

They talked for long hours about their childhoods, about clothes and jewels, all while avoiding the touchy topics of the court and politics. Then they retreated back to their rooms to get ready for dinner.

As Olympias changed into a silver gown lined with a black and gold border, she thought of the lyrical voice Nicesipolis had. No wonder her husband seemed so entranced by her. She had a soothing effect on those around her, including Olympias. She had come here to put her in her place, to cut her enemy down to size, but instead felt as though she had a made a friend.

In the great hall, banners were hung from every corner, and garlands of flowers and ivy hung from the walls. Musicians played as acrobats and dancers performed before the makeshift dais where Phillip sat with a wife on either side of him.

Phillip hid a laugh in his goblet as he regarded the two women talking amiably across him.

Nicesipolis seemed to have worked her magic on Olympias as well. He wondered what rumors would spring out of this public encounter.

The members of the court, who were used to seeing

the serious Olympias sitting calmly on the stool beside her husband, balked as she laughed at her rival's comments.

Phillip, for his part, was content that he did not have to concern himself with the petty fights of women, which could escalate dangerously and require his intervention.

Athens had finally come to the table willing to strike up a treaty of peace with Phillip. Within a few weeks, this Sacred War would come to a close, and Macedonia had squeezed its way to the top.

He had everything he wished for now. Phillip thought happily of resting for a few months in Pella. He had not seen his home in several months and he missed the familiar rooms.

His soldiers were tired too. They needed to return home and recuperate. There was only so much treasure and money that could keep them happy.

There was still Sparta, which stubbornly remained impassive to his threats. His hand clutched his goblet so harshly it seemed ready to crumble. He had written that he would destroy their city and make them all slaves if they didn't submit to him.

Their response? *If. If he succeeded, he could do what he liked.*

Phillip took a few deep breaths to relax. The Spartans were always a foolhardy people, but he was not so sure of his Greek allies to risk waging war against them. The Athenians were likely to switch sides and betray him. No, it was safer to leave them alone for now, as long as they kept out of his way.

But he wouldn't forget. He never forgot.

Pella, 348 BC

The funeral procession was underway, and the hired mourners sent up their wails as they clawed at their hair and clothes.

Phillip did not even hear them. He watched as the dark vault swallowed up his lovely Nicesipolis. Only twenty days ago they had welcomed their pretty little daughter into the world on the same day as his victory at Crocus Field. He had named her Thessalonike to honor the shrieking baby who shouted louder than any soldier he had heard.

Nicesipolis had seemed so happy in those early days and insisted on breastfeeding her child instead of sending her away with a nursemaid.

Now Nicesipolis was dead. Stricken by a fever or infection. The physicians had not been certain and Phillip did not care. All he knew was that she was gone now. His fortunate wife—gone.

He left the funeral before tears could spring from his hardened eyes. He walked past his family but locked eyes with Olympias, whose tears flowed freely for her friend. They shared a private look of sadness, something rare between the pair, who were notorious for their squabbles and fights.

Olympias looked as though she was going to say something but then turned away. She would not leave until she saw that Nicesipolis was honored properly.

Olympias had never had a friend before.

She had loyal companions, but she never felt she could trust them, nor did she regard them with respect. Nicesipolis had wormed her way into her heart, and now she was alone once more.

She thanked the gods for her children, who comforted her with their hugs and kisses. Here were two creatures who relied on her and loved her unconditionally. Alexander was eleven years old now and had already left her side.

He had been placed under the tutelage of Aristotle. Phillip sought to separate her from her son. He believed that she was poisoning him against him, but this did not stop the pair of them from meeting occasionally.

In the privacy of her rooms, he would become her little boy once more and would rest his head in her lap as she stroked his hair and told him stories of glory and heroes that had fallen into myth.

Cleopatra was turning into a little lady. After her tenth birthday, she had shot up like a weed. Now she reached her mother's shoulders. Olympias doted on her pretty daughter and wondered what fantastic match could be made for her. Nothing less than a king would do. Her daughter deserved a kingdom.

For the rest of the month, the city fell into mourning for Nicesipolis. Phillip paid her a great honor and wore black for the entirety of the time.

Slowly regular routines resumed. Life would not hold still for long.

Nicesipolis drifted from memory quickly as Phillip took up his sword again to lead the army against the Ardialoi. Their King Plutarch would prove to be a shrewd commander, and Phillip struggled to win the war. People accused him of being blinded by the loss of Nicesipolis, but Olympias rolled her eyes. She was confident Plutarch would be defeated eventually. Not every victory would come easily, but she supposed at least they weren't whispering that Phillip had lost the gods' favor. That would have been worse.

When word reached Olympias that Phillip's leg had been badly injured on the battlefield, she shuddered. The physicians had to stitch up a deep wound that had cut to the bone. By a stroke of luck a major artery had not been hit, but it was close.

In coded letters they admitted they were not sure if he would be able to walk properly again, much less fight.

Olympias bit her lip as she trudged down the halls toward Alexander's rooms. He was still too young to take on the responsibility of a kingdom. Ever since his father had left for war she had called him to stay with her. It was an effort to protect him and ensure she would be close by to guide him if Phillip perished on the battlefield. Contrary to popular belief, she did not want Phillip dead.

She was nearly to his rooms when a maidservant rushing around ran into her, a crying baby in her arms. When she saw who she had run into, she began quaking at her indiscretion.

"I am sorry, my queen." She bowed low, hiding the child. "Please forgive me."

Olympias blinked. She was not angry but did tend to get annoyed by clumsy slaves. "You should not run while holding a baby. It is irresponsible of you. Whose child is that?"

"It is Lady Nicesipolis's child. I was taking her to her wet nurse. I nearly forgot it was time to feed her," she admitted, blushing red under Olympias's disapproving gaze.

"Give her to me." Olympias held out her hands and accepted the baby.

The little girl cooed in her arms and seemed to settle in as though she belonged there. Olympias began walking away down the hall, leaving a dumbstruck servant behind.

"My lady?"

"Your inadequate services are no longer required. I shall take care of this little princess myself."

Fortuna had smiled on the child, who would have otherwise fallen into oblivion.

Pella, 340 BC

"Thessa! Come out right now." Cleopatra scrambled around the room trying to catch her half-sister.

They were supposed to be getting ready for Cynane's wedding, but as always Thessalonike had escaped from her grasp and now they were sure to be late.

She did not know how her mother had tamed this little creature, but Olympias seemed to be the only one who could get her to behave.

Cleopatra heard a giggle coming from a basket and lifted the lid. She did not give Thessa another chance to run away.

Grasping her young charge with both arms, she hauled her out.

"We need to get you ready. What will Father say if you show up looking like a wild animal?"

The threat did not seem to affect Thessalonike, who was confident in her father's love.

"He won't. He lets Cynane fight and wrestle. Why wouldn't he let me be a wild animal?" She giggled.

Cleopatra sighed and tried again. "I'll tell Mother then, and she won't take you with us when we go visit the temple at Aigai."

The girl's lower lip began to tremble.

"Will you promise to behave? I might even give you a few bangles to wear."

Thessa nodded. "I promise."

Cleopatra set her back down on the cool marble floor and led her back to the bathhouse.

Handmaidens scrubbed their skin until it was pink and then used sweet-smelling oil to massage away the tension in their backs and soothe any dry skin. By the time they left, both royal siblings were completely refreshed and smelled of roses.

Cleopatra had laughed as Thessa squirmed when the maids tickled her, but she had not tried to run away again. If it wasn't for constantly having to ply her with promises and presents, Cleopatra would have loved her half-sister. She was ten years her senior, so it was hardly surprising she couldn't seem to tolerate her childish antics.

"She will teach you patience and give you practice if you have children of your own someday." Olympias had patted her daughter on the head when she complained.

Once they were back in Cleopatra's room, Thessa sat patiently on a stool while her sister sifted through the various chests containing her clothes. She pulled out several options, holding them up to a hammered-out silver mirror to see which would suit her best.

Finally, she settled on a bright yellow himation gown with a silver girdle encrusted with amber beads.

Then, calling over Thessalonike, she sifted through a different set of chests. She picked out a blue gown and a pale green gown for the little princess.

"Which would you like?"

"That one." Thessalonike pointed to the green one.

Cleopatra added two thin gold bangles to her wrists and made her promise to be careful with them. Then she stood back admiring her little sister. She was only eight-years-old, but in her finery and jewels she looked regal and took on the refined appearance her station required.

The two sisters had their hair braided by slaves and then they went off to the hall where the wedding ceremony would take place.

Cynane was nineteen, and by normal standards she was considered old to be getting married for the first time, but she wasn't like any other girl. Her mother was an Illyrian princess and had raised her daughter in the Illyrian fashion.

She spent more time on horseback than she did at her loom. Her chests contained weapons and leather, not jewels and silks. Finally, she had been convinced to settle down. Her father's choice was her cousin, Amyntas Lyncestes. Phillip could have easily seen him as a rival. In fact, Amyntas had been a puppet king before Phillip took the crown, but he had never held it against the boy, who had proven his loyalty over and over again.

Amyntas belonged on the plains, training cavalry and breeding horses. Phillip thought he would be a good match for his warrior daughter. Not only would she bring him and his family closer into the fold, but he had also promised to contribute soldiers to his next campaign.

He was getting tired of whispers of rebellion and assassinations within his own family.

Cleopatra had teased her older sister that she had agreed to the match because Amyntas had stolen her heart with his bright blue eyes and handsome smile. Cynane had thrown a scroll at her and returned to writing out the lineage of one of her great Illyrian ancestors.

The atrium and hall were filled with wedding guests. Some were already teetering from all the wine they had consumed.

Servants were quick to remove such guests before they caused any trouble.

Cleopatra led Thessalonike to the end of the room. A large table had been set up at the end of the room for the royal family to be served from, and she sat her younger sister down on a cushion. After commanding her to sit still, she took her seat beside her.

Philinna was already there but had taken a seat as far back as she could manage. She was one of Phillip's wives, but she was shy and hated large public affairs. She kept to her own rooms and seemed content to weave linen all day. Her son Phillip was also there. He had a dumb expression on his face as he surveyed the crowd and eyed the pretty dancers with unconcealed lust.

He reminded Cleopatra of a child sometimes, but he wasn't as stupid as some people thought and he was strong. Olympias would have surely regarded him as a rival to Alexander, but she barely paid him any attention. Hardly anyone did.

Soon a hush fell over the crowd as Phillip strode in, dressed in his finery and wearing a gold laurel crown on his head. The Thessalian League had awarded him this crown years ago after he had fought and won the third Sacred War. Apollo's champion.

He rarely wore the crown expect for special occasions.

After him followed her own mother, Olympias. Once again she managed to steal everyone's breath away. She was wearing a brilliant blue silk gown, twin gold snake bracelets winding up both arms from her wrists almost to her elbow. Her blond hair had been braided into a crown on her head, pinned there by sapphire quartz pins that sparkled against the lamps as she strode through the room.

Her mother was nearly thirty-five, but she was as beautiful as a goddess.

Phillip honored Olympias with the seat by his side as his official consort and the mother of his heir, though they hardly spoke these days. His other four wives shuffled in after Olympias, but none of them captured the crowd's attention like she had.

Olympias turned around and met Cleopatra's gaze. She regarded her daughter, who was now nearly grown up herself, and wondered how long she would have with her before she was married as well. Then her eyes fell upon Thessalonike, who was already yawning from boredom. After the ceremony, her nursemaid would sweep her away to her rooms to rest. She was too young for public affairs but too old to remain hidden in her rooms.

The priest arrived wearing his plain white linen—a stark contrast to the rest of the gathered crowd in their deep colors. Then Amyntas, with his family trailing behind him, entered, soon followed by Cynane and her mother.

The marriage ceremony was conducted without much pomp, and the bride and groom were quickly wed to the cheering of the gathered guests.

For once Cynane looked like a proper lady, dressed in a brilliant scarlet red gown and red veil. She had even worn a diadem for the occasion. Usually, she detested wearing too much finery, even though her own mother relished in it, but the occasion called for it.

Her groom was a handsome man only six years her senior. Cynane knew very little about him except that he was wealthy. However, he had not complained after she told him that she knew her way around weapons nor when she said that she planned on one day leading her own soldiers into battle alongside her father.

He had not laughed and brushed her aside as others did. It was for this reason that she had agreed to marry him.

Now that the ceremony was done, platters piled high with delicacies poured into the room, carried by slaves dressed in clean white linen.

Thessalonike grabbed greedily at the honeyed dates and figs. She loved sweets.

"Don't eat like an animal," Cleopatra hissed as quietly as she could. Thessalonike retorted by sticking out her tongue at her. Unfortunately, her father had caught sight of the exchange and, scowling, motioned for her to come to him.

Setting aside her food, she walked over to him, head down in penance.

Phillip regarded his daughter coolly until she looked away from his gaze, and then he picked her up and swung her in the air, making her squeal in delight.

"You spoil her," Olympias warned him from his other side.

"Ha. You are the one who spoils her the most." Phillip

set his daughter down on his lap. Even she didn't miss the biting tone he used when addressing his wife.

He smiled again as he regarded the young dark-haired child. "Now try to act like a lady, or I'll have you fed to the lions."

"Yes, Father." She surprised him by wrapping her arms around his middle before sliding down and returning to her seat beside Cleopatra.

Thessalonike was often torn between her adoptive mother and her father. She had a fierce love for both of them, but it was becoming apparent to her that they were enemies. The earliest memories she had of them was of them fighting. She didn't even know why they fought, but several clay pots and cups always shattered when they did.

After seeing Thessa hiding behind a pillar after a bad dream, Olympias had pulled her into her strong arms and rocked her as she sung her a lullaby.

It was Phillip who had taken her for a ride when she had stumbled out in the paddock trailing after Cynane one day. She had escaped her nursemaid and followed after her eldest half-sister, eager to get a look at the horses.

When she saw her father astride his warhorse, she had lifted her arms up to him to be picked up. He had surprised her by complying and holding her in front of him. He had spurred the horse forward into a gallop that left her screaming with delight. Even Cynane had laughed.

These moments were not frequent, but they were enough to fill Thessalonike with adoration for her parents and loyalty to both of them.

After the food was taken away, Thessa was led away back to her rooms. She did not protest, not wishing to make a scene, but she was too excited to sleep.

Her nursemaid had been distracted too, and she was able to slip away. She made her way down the hall to Olympias's own rooms.

She loved being here usually. Olympias would let her play with her jewels and even let her pet her snakes. She had shown her how to pick them up and how to tell apart the deadly ones from the ones she did not have to worry about. Thessa was fascinated by them. Their smooth scales were always cool to the touch.

She peeked into one of the baskets where old Kelainos was resting. He barely moved as she reached in to pet him, whispering the magic spell Olympias had taught her.

The spell was, in fact, nothing more than a soothing prayer that the snakes had all become accustomed too. They could not hear well but recognized the vibrations and knew this was no threat.

Despite what others believed, these were tame snakes. Accustomed to life in the palace, having been hand-raised since they were very young by Olympias or her servants.

Thessalonike believed the rumors that her mother was a sorceress, but she did not fear her. Olympias would never harm her. In her childish heart, she wished that Olympias would teach her how to weave spells too and scry over her silver bowl.

Exploring the nooks and crannies of the room took her a few hours. She found lots of little things to amuse herself with. A bead that had fallen behind a couch cushion, a red scarf. There were countless treasures for her to play with.

Finally getting tired, Thessa made her way over to the large bed. She hoped Olympias would not send her away tonight.

As she got close she heard a hissing sound coming

from the bed. It was a strange sound unlike the sound the other snakes she knew well made. She approached more cautiously. Sometimes strange snakes would find their way inside the palace rooms, and you always had to be careful to avoid getting bitten.

Slowly she pulled back the sheet, struggling with it in her hands.

Curled up on the bed was a strange snake. Its beady eyes blinked at her, its forked tongue flicking the air. Thessa examined it from afar, not making any sudden movements so she wouldn't startle the beast.

"Who are you, darling?" she intoned, swaying back and forth like Olympias had taught her. With some snakes, repetitive motions and soft melodic tones were all they needed to relax them. She had never seen this type of snake before, but she sensed it was dangerous. The diamond pattern on its back and the horned scales above its eyes gave it a devilish appearance.

Just then Olympias appeared, her maids trailing behind her. She had left the feast a bit early, having gotten into another little fight with Phillip, and had not wished to remain. She was surprised to find Thessalonike in her room standing before her bed, a sheet in one hand.

The girl did not look up when she entered the room and seemed frozen.

Taking the hint that something was wrong, Olympias approached her cautiously. At her feet coiled up in a tight ball was a snake. Not just any snake from the looks of it, but an Egyptian viper.

Olympias's hand flashed down before either Thessa or the snake could blink. Her hand grasped the viper by the head while the other one grabbed around its middle. She was an expert at dealing with snakes, even the poisonous variety.

"Everything is fine now, Thessa." She motioned for her maids to check the rest of the room as she carried the struggling viper over to where she kept her other snakes. She stuffed the viper into an empty container, making sure to seal the lid. It was probably hungry and would have to be fed. This snake had been placed here in an assassination attempt and had likely been starved to make it more vicious.

She scowled, thinking of what she'd like to do to the people who had done this. She wasn't worried for herself, but little Thessa could have been the unwitting victim.

Thessa was approaching her with a questioning look on her face. She was too young to realize the truth of the situation.

"What are you doing out of bed, little one?" Olympias scooped her up in her arms and Thessa wrapped her arms around her neck.

"I couldn't sleep, and then I snuck in here and found the snake."

"Don't worry about him. He was just looking for a home, but you did well to not move or scream." She placed her down on her bed. "We'll train him to be nice and calm. I'll show you how to manage him."

She smiled at the little girl, who nodded and yawned, suddenly feeling very tired.

Olympias sat beside her until she was fast asleep before getting up off the bed. Fortuna had smiled upon her once more. It was not the first time this thread of thought had struck her, nor would it be the last.

Her maids seemed terrified by how she would react. They knew what that snake meant.

"Niobe, go try to find out who was behind this. Bribe who you must." She turned to her other servants. "We must be alert. They will likely try again until they are caught."

She spent the next two days with the viper. Together with her maids, she extracted its venom so for a while, at least, its bite would not be deadly. Olympias treated it like a child. Feeding and cooing over it day and night until it finally allowed her to pick it up without any complaint and sat contently wrapped around her arms. It would never be as tame as some of her other snakes, but this would be sufficient for what she had planned next.

On the third day, she strode through the hall with it wrapped around her arms as calmly as though it had been one of her gold bangles. The crowd gasped and moved away when they noticed the viper. There was no mistaking the deadly creature.

Phillip gaped at her and demanded to know what she was doing.

"Someone left me a present in my room," she responded calmly. "Thessalonike found it." She whispered this last part to him and his eyes narrowed, understanding what she meant. She doubted that he would have made much fuss about an assassination attempt on her, but he loved his daughter as any father would.

Then Olympias took her seat at his side and addressed the crowd. "I would like to thank whoever gave me this gift. It is such a rare creature." She stroked the back of the viper's head and the crowd recoiled again.

Her sharp eyes caught the sneering look that passed between Attalus and Lycander. She did not react. Not yet.

There was something so unnatural about her.

That night Niobe confirmed that it had been Lycander's men who had visited the market and made an unusual purchase.

"Efficient as always, Niobe. I have my suspicions as well. I know Attalus must be behind this as well, but my husband would not move against him. I guess I'll have to satisfy myself with Lycander." She tutted and began plotting her revenge.

Lycander returned from the training yard exhausted and covered in a sheen of sweat. He would go to the bathhouse shortly after he picked up a change of clothes and left his armor at home. Usually, a servant was with him, but his usual manservant had fallen ill this morning and rather than trusting someone else with this important task he did it himself.

As he stepped into the courtyard, he could hear the cries of his son from inside the house.

"Quiet him down," he shouted, but there was no response and his son kept crying. Annoyed, he threw off his leather plate and laid his shield and sword against the wall carefully.

He entered the pavilion to find the slave girl huddled and trembling in the corner, as white as a ghost.

"What is it, girl?" He wanted to slap her. She didn't say a word and he shook her.

Her head lolled and then she fell to the floor, her body still shaking. He noticed the white foam coming out of her mouth.

"Poison!" He stepped back from her. For the first time,

he noticed the eerie silence of the house, save for the cries of his son. He did not spare her a second glance, or any of the other slaves convulsing or already dead around the house as he ran for his son's rooms.

In the cradle of his crying son was a snake. Its fangs embedded deep in the child's leg. With a flash of his dagger the snake's head was lopped off. It twitched in the cradle as he picked up his son and removed the snake's head.

The wound bled, but he saw that the snake was not poisonous. His son would survive.

He kissed the bawling babe and clutched at him as he went to look for his wife.

She was in the inner courtyard, slumped over in her seat by the loom. He stepped away from the sight. What madness had fallen across his house? What curse?

Unbidden, a pair of gray eyes flashed in his mind and he realized immediately who had done this. He swallowed hard, looking down at his son. Was she satisfied with the price she'd exacted from him? Was that witch finished with him? He did not think so. Olympias was always thorough in her revenge.

He left his house carrying his son and a purse filled with coins and jewels. He grabbed his sword and headed to his friend's house. He would have to go into hiding or beg Attalus to give him protection.

Why hadn't their plan succeeded? He cursed at the gods. Had he not been careful? How could they protect such a witch?

Lycander never made it out his front door.

Choking, he collapsed to the dirt floor in the courtyard as an arrow pierced his neck. He looked up and thought he saw the figure of a woman. "My son..." The blood gurgled in his throat as he prayed for mercy, and his vision went dark.

Olympias relished the way Attalus would flinch at every sound for weeks.

Rumors broke out over what happened to Lycander—snakes had descended upon his household or Zeus had struck them down at her request. They were ridiculous, but no one dared point a finger at Olympias, not that she would have cared. She had not been the one to poison the wine and food or the one to shoot the arrow.

Let them whisper if they wanted to. This was not the first time she had done Phillip's dirty work for him, nor would it be the last.

Her cruel efficiency often scared him as well. She liked to extract a heavy fine from her enemies. It taught them a lesson and made her friends think twice about stabbing her in the back.

Phillip had seen the necessity of this, although he would have preferred a public trial, but this struck fear into the hearts of his enemies more than a simple execution would have.

Attalus was struck down a peg or two.

Thessalonike was ignorant to all of this. She played with her nursemaids and followed after Cleopatra day and night as though nothing was wrong. She did not notice the servants being extra careful around her or the stares she got from courtiers.

Olympias had let everyone know that if a hair was harmed on her head, they would be answerable to her.

Aigai, 336 BC

Blood. It was everywhere these days.

Draining into the sand of the execution ground, staining tapestries and flowing down stairwells.

Carrying the blood of Phillip of Macedonia in your veins had become a crime. The only way to repent was to die.

Alexander of Macedonia had claimed his throne, and now he sought to cleanse his realm of pretenders and rivals.

No one was spared.

Overnight, many of her relatives began disappearing. Those whom she had called uncles, cousins, brothers, and sisters were gone, and now in her dreams she drowned in their blood.

Thessalonike did not like leaving her rooms. From her window, she heard screaming. At her doorway, she heard the hurried footsteps of those fleeing or the guards marching past with their latest arrest.

She trembled alone in her rooms, desperate for some sense of normalcy. But for the moment, she was forgotten and there would be no comfort for her.

Just weeks before, Thessa had been dressed in her new gown for Cleopatra's wedding to the king of Epirus. She played the lyre for her father and the wedding guests, blushing when they applauded her efforts.

They had returned from exile for this wedding. Olympias, Cleopatra, Alexander, and she had all been living away from Phillip and his household for two years now. Ever since he had married Attalus's niece. Phillip adored his new wife as much as Olympias hated her.

When Phillip declared that his new wife would give him a true heir to his throne, Thessalonike had left with Olympias to go into exile. She had missed her father every day.

Finally, their family had seemed to reconcile over Cleopatra's wedding.

Then Pausanias plunged the dagger into her father's heart and her world came tumbling down.

The men hired to protect you could just as easily kill you. That's what she learned that day. Your family was your greatest ally and enemy—she learned that the next day.

Phillip had wanted his new son by Eurydice to be king, but he was just a baby and had died at Olympias's command. He had been too dangerous to be left alive.

Europa had not been. She was only a year old, but Olympias wanted to eradicate the daughter of her rival and she had her buried alongside her mother. Their uncle, Attalus, suffered a likewise horrible death, though by the time he was executed he welcomed the stroke of the sword that lopped off his head.

Thessalonike wished to go back to the time when her father would take her riding. When she was pampered by slaves and rocked in Olympias's warm embrace. Now her world seemed empty.

"Father," she whispered as the tears rolled down her cheeks. She should have been impassive, like Cleopatra. She should have been stronger like Cynane and braver like Alexander. But she had too much of her mother's sweet nature in her, so she hid in her rooms, not letting anyone get too near.

They might be hiding a dagger.

Pella, 333 BC

"Can you see anything?"

Thessalonike pulled away from the silver bowl and shook her head. "Nothing."

"That's all right. Most times the gods do not grace us with visions." Olympias patted her hands.

"They seem to favor you." Thessalonike frowned. She desired to have the power Olympias seemed to possess. She was willing to learn, but it seemed the gods had other plans in store for her.

"Patience." Olympias sighed. She was getting too old to be dealing with energetic youth. Thessalonike never seemed to be able to sit still. Yet, as her only remaining child, she was precious to her.

Alexander was laying siege to Tyre now. She hoped to hear news from her ambitious son any day now saying that he had been victorious.

The early years of his reign had been tumultuous, but

he made his enemies cleave to him. The gods had given him victory after victory. They were calling him divine now. With his golden hair and fair skin, he looked more like the son of Zeus than the son of Phillip.

Neither Olympias nor Alexander dispelled these rumors. It suited them to create an illustrious heritage. He was building an empire.

That first year had been tough on Thessalonike. She had nightmares for months, would not touch her food and seemed to be wasting away.

Olympias, assured of her son's position and her own power, had finally taken notice and was shocked to find her so ill.

Under her love and tutelage, she had regained some of her old exuberance.

Thessa was no longer an innocent child. She had turned fifteen and was becoming a woman, though Olympias said she still had some growing to do.

The violence she had witnessed years ago seemed a dim memory now, but she still quaked at the sight of blood and she had become deathly afraid of water. She had dreamed too often that year of drowning, and now she could barely manage sitting still in the bathhouse while the maids scrubbed the dirt from her skin.

There was also another difference between her and the rest of her remaining family. Secretly, Thessalonike harbored a deep resentment toward Alexander. She blamed him for everything.

When she was younger, she was jealous of the attention given to him by both Phillip and Olympias. Now she was angry at the praise he was getting for destroying those around him. She knew that all kings should be great warriors, but she did not forget how he had ordered the execution of his little brother, his cousins.

Where was the glory in that? What honor was there in murdering innocents?

She also knew better than to say a word of this to Olympias. She did not hate nor ill-wish her fortunate brother, and he kept them safe.

Her attention had lately been turned to learning to scry using the silver bowl like Olympias did. Occasionally, visions of the future would come to Olympias through the bowl and she wished to learn how to do this as well. She wanted to escape the present and flee to the distant future, which she imagined to be bright and cheerful.

There were other useful things for her to learn as well. Potions and spells. All within her grasp if she wished.

This was what she flung herself into now. Studying the great mysteries that Olympias seemed to command. She wanted power and protection—she would get it.

Her lazy summer days were interrupted by the arrival of the news of Alexander's recent victories.

The city awaited the wagons filled with jewels and money that were to follow in a great triumphant parade.

Macedonia would celebrate this latest victory in style. Even the dour Antipater seemed to be cheerful and for once agreed with Olympias that games would have to be held to honor the soldiers who had fought.

The messenger promised Olympias that Alexander had sent a personal gift and a chest filled with treasure—from gold chains to little silver statues. Then there were the slaves captured as well. Good workers were always in short supply.

"You shall have your pick, Thessa," Olympias promised

her. "You are old enough now and you should have your own slave."

Thessalonike wasn't sure if she liked the idea. Wouldn't whoever she chose hate her? She still feared knives in the dark.

"Egypt will fall," Thessalonike predicted one day after returning from listening in on a meeting with Olympias. Alexander was planning to conquer this kingdom as well now that Tyre was out of the way.

Olympias heard petitions alongside Antipater, who was acting as the official regent and general while Alexander was away. She enjoyed sharing news with Thessalonike, who she called her little scribe.

"I am sure you are right," she agreed.

She had been frustrated that Antipater had been given so much power. She disliked the barrel-chested general who could not be budged from his decisions once they were set.

Thessalonike liked to joke at times that once he knew Olympias's opinion he would purposely choose the opposite just to oppose her.

He looked down on Olympias, not only for being a woman but for her ambitions and her machinations early on in her son's reign. He regarded assassination and lewd behavior with disdain, and Olympias represented both. She did not fit in his neat little world.

Thessalonike found their bickering amusing but couldn't help but remember what had happened to Attalus. He too had been Olympias's enemy—would she also raze Antipater and his dynasty to the ground? She did not think so. She knew his son Cassander was one of Alexander's closest advisors. They had grown up and studied together. Now they fought side by side, plotted battle strategies and drank together.

In truth, she was jealous Alexander had so many companions around him while she felt so alone.

❀

Pella, 332 BC

The news had shocked Olympias as much as it had shocked Thessalonike.

Alexander had betrothed her to Hephaestion during the siege of Gaza. He had also crushed Tyre and now seemed poised to capture the rest of Egypt. The news arrived with the latest messenger, scrolled in haste at the bottom in Alexander's own hand so there could be no mistake.

Thessalonike was proud that she had not cried nor complained when Olympias had told her, even though she had her own reservations.

Later, Olympias came to her rooms and they spoke frankly, away from the eyes and ears of the courtiers. For Alexander, they would provide a united front. It was crucial for peace to be maintained.

"I cannot marry a man who will be away at war for years. Nor can I share a man with Alexander," Thessalonike admitted.

Olympias sighed. She agreed, of course. Besides, there were better men out there for Thessalonike to wed. Hephaestion was her son's favorite now, his lands and fortunes made in his service, but he did not come from an illustrious family, nor could he bring an alliance with a great family.

More than ever, Alexander needed to cement alliances by bringing them into the fold.

Tucking a stray strand of hair behind her adopted daughter's ears, she hushed her and told her all would be well.

"This is not the end. I have my own reservations about the match. Give it time. Alexander will change his mind and you shall see how quickly things can change."

Thessalonike met the cold gray eyes and searched them for signs. "How do you know? Have you seen something?"

The older woman laughed. "I was engaged several times before marrying. I do not need magic to know that betrothals can be broken. Nothing is forever." She urged her to flip around and began taking apart Thessalonike's braided hair. Grabbing a comb, she pulled it through the dark locks, untangling them for bed.

"Do you think of him?" Thessalonike was always hesitant to bring up Phillip, but she had loved her father and didn't understand Olympias's hatred of him.

"I try not to." Her tone was now cheerful, but Thessalonike knew enough to drop the subject. Unfortunately, Olympias seemed keen on erasing Phillip from her life altogether. She was even encouraging the rumors that Alexander was the son of Zeus.

The people were more than happy to lap up this propaganda. Alexander's constant victories over the Persians and other foreigners only seemed to cement them further. He won when the odds were stacked against him. It seemed as though no one could stand in his way.

But Thessalonike had seen behind the curtain. It was Alexander's ministers, mother, and commanders like Antipater that held the threads of the kingdom together. It would be easy for it to unravel.

This is treason, a voice in her head spoke, reminding her to never voice her thoughts.

Sometimes she imagined what she would do if this happened. She would pack her bags with treasure and ride her horse to some distant provincial town in Thessaly, claiming to be the daughter of some dead noble, and live out her life in peace.

She knew that things would never go so smoothly. There was no outrunning war. Just years before, Alexander had razed Thebes to the ground.

She had never been to Thebes herself, but she had heard plenty of things about the once mighty city. Now Alexander had torn down its walls and set fire to the city. Its men and women turned into slaves.

Thessalonike shivered, but she supposed there were worse punishments.

"Will you come with me to the theater tomorrow?" Olympias asked her. She tried not to command her. Thessalonike always seemed to chafe under commands. Olympias studied the back of her head.

She was a walking contradiction. On one hand she was tough and had proved herself to be quite intelligent. On the other, she was quick to quiver in fright and seemed to carry a bitterness about her that one so young should not have.

She did not understand the need to kill one's enemies. She was too kind. Olympias sighed out loud. She hoped the girl would never have to learn that sometimes it was necessary to commit such acts. She suspected that the girl harbored a fear of her now or perhaps even resentment, but she loved her with all her heart.

Those days after Phillip's death she had been alone with shadows and her own thoughts. They seemed to have chipped away at her naïveté. Olympias regretted not looking after her better then but had since taken her under her wing. The girl wanted for nothing and Olympias, who had raised her since she was a baby, regarded her as her own child.

"What is it?"

Olympias was pulled out of her thoughts. "I am jealous of your dark hair when my own is turning gray and white."

"To match your eyes better." Thessalonike was quick with compliments and Olympias kissed the back of her head.

"Sleep well tonight."

Not much changed for Thessalonike following her betrothal. There was not much for her to do other than making the standard public gestures of thanks and good luck.

It was several months before she even heard from Hephaestion when he sent her a small gift and asked after her health. She was ashamed of herself for not taking the initiative sooner.

The triumphant procession had finally arrived, parading through the city and up to the palace gates. Thessalonike had watched from the parapets as chests of treasure, carts of spices, silks, and other precious objects soon filled the courtyard, illuminating the usually dusty area with sparkling gems and brilliant carpets.

Slaves were also carted in. The best picks were sent to

the palace to let them choose who they wished.

Olympias had been in need of a new body slave and had decided that Thessalonike needed a companion. She could choose among these slaves. There was a learning opportunity for her here.

Thessalonike followed at her heels in a gray himation gown.

She eyed the slave women suspiciously. Would these women kill her if they had the chance? Her brother had enslaved them. She questioned them one by one, asking where they came from and what they could do. They were surprised she knew their dialect, but Thessalonike had a gift for learning.

Finally, she settled on a short Egyptian named Aya, who had been a royal slave in Tyre. Her plump form gave her a matronly appearance, even though she was only in her early twenties.

Aya had been a slave all her life and there was little danger of her rebelling or not knowing how to behave.

She was adaptable, and unlike many of the others who had come from Tyre, she did not hold grudges against her captors. Then again, she had not had any children or lovers that had been murdered by the invaders.

Still, Aya possessed a sharp tongue that luckily seemed to entertain Thessalonike endlessly.

She had once served the queen, and now she would serve a princess. Aya made a joke that she had been demoted. Thessa laughed and knew she would like her new companion.

"The gods made me a slave, but just as quickly they can switch our places," she teased Thessalonike one day at the bathhouse.

"That is true. Have you ever heard the story of Oedipus? The son of a king was abandoned and raised as a peasant but becomes a king in the end."

"Yes, and in the end, he suffers a terrible fate." Aya made a circle with her finger. "Fortuna's wheel never stops spinning."

Thessalonike copied the motion. "Is this a spell?" She had still not lost her childish fascination with magic, though she did not seem to possess an ounce of it in her entire body.

"No." Aya shook her head. "It's a reminder that no matter how high you climb, you will fall."

"I should have your tongue cut out." She was already a princess. There was not much higher she could climb, so what was next? The fall? Thessa shivered at the thought.

Aya laughed. "Don't worry, mistress, some people will never move on the wheel. For example, I shall remain at the bottom of Fortuna's wheel. I have grown accustomed to my position."

Thessalonike joined her in her laughter. "You aren't that ugly. Perhaps a prince will fall in love with you, but I suppose you are right. It is safer to be you instead of me." She thought of Europa, who had been such a little child and had been killed because of whose daughter she was.

A body slave approached with oils for her skin and hair, and she allowed her to massage the various concoctions into her skin.

Out of the corner of her eye, she watched with interest as Aya shaved her scalp with trained steady motions. She did not cut herself even once. The first time Aya had requested anything of her mistress had been to see if she might be allowed to wear a wig and shave her head.

Thessalonike knew very little of Egyptian culture but knew that the elite followed such customs. She was horrified at the thought of cutting her hair. She didn't let it grow too long, but neither did she shave her head. So out of curiosity, she surprised Aya one day with a glossy black wig braided with red and black beads at the bottom.

Now it was a common practice to see Aya shaving her head. It did keep lice away from her and made her stand out in the palace. Everyone called her the Princess's Egyptian.

It was Aya who delivered Hephaestion's letter to her three months later.

Thessalonike was confused by its sudden arrival after so many months. He did not elaborate too much but hoped she was well. He also promised to send her betrothal gift and apologized for not doing so sooner.

She had not even noticed this breach in etiquette and wondered if it would seem rude to write to him saying there was no need for him to do such a thing. She did not know much about him, and while she could always ask the slaves or bribe the messengers, she had very little interest in him.

In the end, she replied to him with a curt thank-you and did not embellish the letter further other than asking him to send Alexander her love and well-wishes.

Aya was curious to hear of her illustrious brother, but Thessalonike did not have much to tell her. Yes, he was just as tall and beautiful as was rumored. Did the sun seem to shine brighter when he was nearby? No. Did he possess a golden aura that surrounded him? No.

In truth, she had rarely seen her famous half-brother at all. They lived together when she was very young, but by the time she was walking he was off getting tutored by Aristotle. By the time she was attending social functions, he was off leading legions of men against his father's enemies.

Still, he was kind to her when he remembered her. Sometimes he would send her special little gifts just for her. Once it had been a vial containing water gathered from the fountain of youth—that's what the scroll claimed.

Thessalonike had smiled and used it to wash her hair. The water was perfumed with the scent of myrrh and it was likely nothing special, but she loved that Alexander had bothered to remember that she loved these little things—magical baubles and charms. Another time he had a brooch fashioned for her with the Vergina Sun embossed on it. She liked trailing her fingers over the rays of the sun, counting them each in her head.

As Thessalonike was being entertained by her new companion and trying to take an active part in the spring festivals and games by purchasing her own set of horses and chariots to race in the upcoming Olympic Games, she had not noticed the grim expression constantly present on Olympias's face or the frustrated look of Antipater as he ruled the council.

Normally, she'd be trying to eavesdrop or question Olympias until she pulled the truth out of her. As it was, she was oblivious until one day at the market she noticed a well-dressed man with a sword at his belt seeming to follow her and Aya as they walked through the crowds of merchants and customers.

Thessalonike liked to slip away to do shopping for herself rather than send out someone to fetch something for her. Aya had scolded her for this habit, saying that it was better left to slaves, but did not complain about the exercise.

It was from Aya that Thessalonike learned that other kingdoms and empires regarded Macedonia as a backwater province. She remembered how her father's dinners would be social affairs with bawdy jokes and uncouth people.

Aya spoke of calm collected banquets where women would be kept separate from the men during most occasions. Thessalonike was intrigued and always asked Aya to tell her more stories of distant lands and their customs.

Now she leaned over, pretending to investigate a wool scarf, and asked her if she noticed the man following them.

"Aya, why is that man following us?" Thessalonike asked her before moving away. They weaved their way through the market of Thessaly as shopkeepers called out to them with their wares.

Aya looked behind them and spotted a sullen man who seemed to be tracing their steps.

He did not look like an assassin; however, he wasn't wearing the garb of a soldier either.

"Perhaps we should ask him," Aya suggested. Her fingers touched the hilt of the small knife she carried with her. It was her duty to protect her mistress.

Thessalonike surprised the man by stopping suddenly and turning to meet his gaze.

"Hello," she greeted him as he approached, waiting to see how he would react.

He coughed, embarrassed, and bowed at the waist in respect. "Who are you?" She arched her eyebrow, taking in his broad shoulders and lean muscles. He had to be a soldier.

"I am Maro, son of Faeus. I was instructed to look out for your safety. I am sorry, Princess."

"By who?" She interrupted him but saw that some of the shopkeepers had heard him address her as royalty, and the whispers carried through the crowd.

"Lady Olympias."

"Ah." That made sense. Thessalonike had been adamant that she did not want guards following her around everywhere she went while she was in Pella. She distrusted them and had not seen the need. She wasn't important enough to assassinate. At the moment, there were bigger fish to fry.

"Well, you might as well walk beside me then. Instead of frightening my maid by following us around like a man hiding something." Aya didn't contradict her. It had been Thessa who was scared.

Maro saluted the young princess and took a spot beside her.

She drew much more attention now. Before she had been a rich lady walking with her maid through the market. Now with a soldier as well, her importance was more evident.

The shopkeepers called out more insistently to her, wishing to get the patronage of an important lady.

"Look what you've done, Maro. I can no longer be anonymous. Shall we walk back? You can tell me all about yourself." She smiled up at him, and he was surprised by the way it sent his heart racing.

Was she the type to enjoy stringing a man along? He had seen Alexander the Great once before, and she looked nothing like her golden brother. She was a wispy young woman with dark hair, but her innocent appearance was deceiving, for her eyes gleamed with intelligence and mischief. He was also surprised to find she was nearly as tall as him.

The trio walked in awkward silence for a while until she addressed him again.

"So who are you, Maro? How did you get assigned to be my protector?"

"I am a Thespian. My father was a nobleman, but my mother was a slave girl. When I did not show any promise for the theater or the arts, my father trained me to use a sword. It was my greatest desire to fight alongside Alexander the Great and I left my home."

"And you ended up in the service of his sister," she teased him. The haughty expression on her face mirrored that of Olympias.

"It is an honor."

"You won't win glory with me. Perhaps you should ask to be reassigned. I have no need for a soldier like yourself."

"You are laughing at me." He scowled at the back of her head but hid his expression when she turned around to look at him.

"Perhaps I am. But I am being honest. You'd be put to better use fighting King Agis and his Spartans."

"No, for you see you were right. I am fine with a sword, but I do not have a head for strategy, nor am I favored with strength. I am lucky to have even gotten this post."

She was surprised by his honest reply and studied him closer. It was true he did not appear especially strong. He acted too carefree, unlike the other serious soldiers she had seen. He dreamed of glory, but he was not built for it.

Perhaps he was too embarrassed to say anything. She realized he must still be newly trained without much experience, seeing as he had not been given too much responsibility. But Olympias must have seen something in him to trust him to look after her.

Thessalonike marched straight to Olympias's rooms, having dismissed Maro and Aya.

She entered without a word and took a seat across from her mother as she waited for her to finish instructing the minister on the routes the supply train should take to resupply Alexander.

The ministers always consulted both Olympias and Antipater, not wishing to anger any of them, though of course they deferred to Antipater usually.

Alexander had not declared which side anyone should listen to. He was tired of the constant fighting at home and preferred not to get involved. In response to their questions he had simply shrugged and let them look after his kingdom however they saw fit. In private letters, he did not hold back as much from scolding his mother for creating rifts and begged her to get along with Antipater, whom he trusted and respected greatly. Assured of his love, Olympias continued to do as she pleased.

She now regarded Thessalonike huffing in the corner with amusement. You could read the girl's emotions like a book.

"Come sit beside me, Thessa." She called her over using her nickname.

Thessalonike took a seat before her on a padded cushion and regarded her guardian with exasperation. "Why did you assign Maro to guard me?"

Olympias reached for her unread scrolls and broke the seal to begin reading them. "I simply thought you needed the added protection. I know how you like wandering around the city with only your maid to attend you. At least now I can be assured of your safety."

Thessalonike shook her head. "There's more to it than just that. Why won't you tell me?"

"It is nothing to concern yourself over."

She should have dropped the matter altogether but found she enjoyed being difficult and pressed forward. "I wonder if it has anything to do with Antipater rallying his men."

Olympias practically clamped her hand over her mouth. "Silence. How do you know this?"

Thessalonike shrugged, but when Olympias fixed her with one of her famous glares she quickly recounted how she had been in the stables feeding her horses when Antipater came in from a long ride raving about rations for his army under his breath. "I hid in the stalls and he did not know I was there. I think he thought he was alone. Anyway, I can only assume that meant trouble."

Smirking, Olympias relaxed back into her seat. She put aside her work for now. "You've turned yourself into a little spy. Anyway, I suppose you should know. There have been rumors of uprisings and threats, not only upon Alexander but his family as well. Darius promised support to those who would rise up against your brother. We need to be careful."

She laughed a little. "That old king? He's been chased away by Alexander. What harm could he do?"

"I thought you were smart." Olympias swatted the back of her head. "Even a headless viper is deadly. All he needs to do is sneak some of his assassins into the city or into Alexander's war camp and this war is lost. You don't need an army to do that, so you need protection."

"All right." Thessalonike stood. "I could learn to use a spear like Cynane or a dagger. I'd be good at that."

"No, you wouldn't. You are much too old for that sort of training now, but if you are hungry for learning I can put you to work in my own medicine cabinet."

Thessalonike's eyes widened. She knew what this meant. She would learn to brew potions and how to create little spells.

"But you have to behave and don't give Maro too much trouble. He's a good soldier, and I think he was disappointed when I assigned him to you and did not send him out to Alexander."

"He worships Alexander, but I suppose he shall do his best to protect me in the hopes of getting noticed and promoted." She sighed, seeing the wisdom in Olympias's choice. Loyalty was hard to come by these days.

Over the next few weeks, Thessalonike reported to Olympias's rooms and studied the various scrolls assigned to her. They outlined various medicines and how to make them. Most, she thought with a smile, were poisons for enemies. Olympias's tutelage did not begin with actual practice until she had proved she could memorize the various ingredients and their properties. Additionally, she had to learn how to prepare and handle the concoctions. Other medicines had more innocent purposes, from helping with a headache to preventing a woman from becoming pregnant.

Olympias had collected these over the years, either bought directly from physicians or brought to her by her little spy network. She kept the scrolls under lock and key. As an added protection she had copied the recipes down in a code only she and a few others could read. Now she opened her world to Thessalonike, who proved an avid learner. It also kept her close to home without getting her into too much trouble.

Her education was intensified as she proved herself more capable. Working at the loom now seemed boring to her in comparison to preparing these little potions for Olympias.

"You must not avoid your other chores, Thessalonike," Olympias had scolded her one day as she watched her cut the witch hazel leaves into thin strips to be boiled down.

"This is much more interesting." She shrugged.

"Your husband will not appreciate such rebellious behavior." It had been four months now since her betrothal, and still her wedding date had not been set. She was coming to believe that it would never come, and that suited her just fine.

"I don't care what my husband thinks." Thessalonike shrugged yet again, making Olympias shake her head.

"You are not even of my blood, but you have the same fire in you." She touched Thessalonike's back. "Too bad you are not suited to joining the Cult of Dionysus."

Thessa whipped around to face her. "Why am I not suited? I wish to be just like you. I know you have magic. Why can I not do it too?" It was as though she was a six-year-old child again, begging to be taught.

"It is not so simple. You cannot will yourself to possess magic. We have tried several times to see if the gods have blessed you and they have not. Besides, your temperament is not suited for the order. There are other ways to gain power. You do not need to seem so distraught." Olympias tried to reassure her.

Thessalonike composed herself and returned to the

chopping block. She was going to be helping the slaves in the garden next week, watching how they planted herbs and ingredients needed for Olympias's potions. She would learn to make sure in the future she would know how to direct her own servants to produce the most potent herbs.

"It is a sore subject for you, but don't fret. None of your siblings have this power you seem to covet. Be happy with what you have. This will help you more than anything else." Olympias pointed to the chopping block and knife. "Make sure you go work at your loom after you have washed your hands. I shall ask Aya to make sure you did."

During her lessons, Aya was always sent away, though the woman knew enough to know what was going on. Thessalonike was being tutored by Olympias in her arts and sorcery. She watched for the signs that her mistress had gone down this dark path but for now was happy to see she had not.

It was dangerous meddling with magic, not just because there were side effects but because of how others would perceive you. The rumors around Thessalonike never seemed to take hold though, and Aya wondered if this was proof of some magic of hers.

In truth, Thessalonike had cultivated a calm pleasing demeanor. Her soft features and trusting eyes made all who came across her lulled into a sense of trust and peace. This she had inherited from her birth mother, who she could not remember. Aya knew it would help her in the future if Antipater's hatred of Olympias ever went too far, for the old man seemed to have a soft spot for the princess.

Aigai, 332 BC

The old capital was refreshing. The temperature dropped as the litters carried them high onto the rocky hill where the palace stood. The forests and mountains offered protection from the growing heat.

Olympias had the court moved as Pella became unbearable in the summer heat. Even the ponds and bath-houses had seemed to dry up.

There was another reason for the move. The rumors of dissent had become a well-known fact. Sparta and Athens were in open talks with Darius, and any day now there might be a rebellion. Antipater was trying to come to a diplomatic agreement—knowing full well that victory was not guaranteed.

Alexander was busy celebrating his victories in Egypt. He had conquered the great nation and now they called him Zeus-Ammon after their sun god. He was their libera-tor, even though he had razed several of their cities to the ground. Now he had also funded the building of a great city on the seaside of the Aegean. Regardless, it would take him months, at least, to return with the army, and by then it would be too late anyway. At the moment he was more focused on holding on to the foothold he'd gained in Egypt.

It seemed as though the Macedonians would once again have to face down their enemies without their glorious king.

Thessalonike ended up at the center of these diplo-matic talks. Sparta would be unmovable, but Athens might be persuaded to remain loyal. Antipater had been commu-nicating urgently with several of the key politicians in

Sparta. Phocion, a strategos from one of the oldest noble families, seemed to be the most willing to agree to peace terms. He had an unmarried son and a new treaty would be drawn up.

The marriage of Thessalonike to Phocus would bring Athens closer into the fold of Macedonia.

At first, they had desired Alexander to marry an Athenian woman, but he had remained implacable to his mother's demands. Some vague promises were made that in the future he might take one as his wife, but for now they would have to make do with Thessalonike.

That was Antipater's plan, but Olympias did not trust the Athenians. She had too much intrigue coursing through her veins to believe their promises. So a middle ground was struck between Antipater and Olympias.

They would send Thessalonike to her betrothal ceremony along with one of Antipater's ministers to help get a better idea of where Athens's loyalties truly lay. They would not stop watching their borders to the east, nor cementing their position and preparing for war until the matter was settled.

Olympias sat on her makeshift throne, watching as Thessalonike played the lyre for her. She had a pleasing countenance and Aya provided a strong voice to go along with her melody.

Unknown to Antipater, Olympias was planning to give Thessalonike a task of her own. She could be her own little spy in Athens. After all, they would not suspect a mere woman to be much of a threat.

As the song came to an end, Olympias applauded them.

Setting aside her lyre and wiping the sheen of sweat

from her forehead, Thessalonike came to stand before her mother. "Even here it is hot. Any idea when I am to leave for Athens?"

"Soon enough. Antipater will prepare an escort for you, but you must also keep Maro close to you. Don't run away and get yourself into trouble."

Thessalonike gave her a toothy grin. "I promise I'll try. I am excited to explore. Do you think I'll have the chance to visit the Acropolis?"

"I am sure you will. Now run along and find something else to occupy yourself with. I need some time alone." Thessalonike wondered what spells she was planning on weaving but left without any protest.

Outside the courtyard, Maro was standing at attention and followed behind Aya as they walked past.

"I don't think it shall be long before we are off to Athens." Thessalonike spoke to Maro, who was impatient to set out on this journey. He was eager to get the opportunity to gain some favor. The chance to prove himself in battle was weighing on him, even though Thessalonike always tried to criticize him for one thing or another.

Perhaps he would get the chance to silence her wagging tongue once and for all.

The women went to work at the loom, and he found his thoughts drifting away from him as he stood. He had not realized he was leaning against the wall until her clear voice caused him to jump to attention.

She laughed at his clumsy attempts to catch himself. "You don't seem to possess much stamina, soldier." She teased him mercilessly. Her hands never stopped moving over the threads, weaving the shuttle in and out with expert ease.

He bowed and apologized.

"I think we are safe enough here. Why don't you go to the training yards and see if you can improve your skills?" she suggested lightly, finding the perfect excuse to dismiss him and allow him some freedom too.

"Whatever you say, Lady."

The corners of her mouth turned up in a half smile and she could barely stop herself from laughing again. The other women in the room were already watching them out of the corners of their eyes.

Aya scolded her as she sat beside her, handing her thread. "You are too mean to him. I might accuse you of liking him, if I didn't know how you liked to torment me too."

Thessalonike gave her a nudge in response. "There's something so infuriating about him. He thinks he is too good for me but he's barely competent, so I try to take him down a peg or two." She lied fluidly. In truth, he was not as unskilled as she liked to pretend, and Aya's comment hit too close to home too. She couldn't help it if sometimes she noticed how handsome he looked, not that she would ever stoop so low.

She finished her work faster than she thought would be possible. She was working on a length of fine red cloth with a gold border. This could be fashioned into her wedding gown if she was ever finally married. She had never been given such fine thread before, but after her first betrothal to Hephaestion Olympias had declared she was skilled enough to begin work on finer things.

The work with the thread helped her in other departments as well.

From being able to chop ingredients more precisely to

keeping a steady hand when measuring ingredients, her fingers moved quickly and nimbly at the various tasks. There could be no room for hesitation or imprecision.

The sun was beginning to sink low now and there was no use straining her eyes to continue working.

She stood and Aya followed after her as she made her way down the steps into the courtyard.

"Where are you going?" Aya looked pensive, as though she suspected.

"To the training yard. Perhaps we'll catch a sparring match."

"It is unseemly for you to go," Aya reminded her, but Thessalonike shot her a pointed stare.

"I am the sister of Alexander, son of Zeus-Ammon. Nothing I do is unseemly." She hurried her pace, forcing the shorter woman to practically jog to keep up with her.

"If I tell your mother, then we'll see who gets punished," Aya muttered under her breath, but she was making empty threats. She had been with Thessalonike for a year now and she liked the exuberant child. She was seven years her junior and while sometimes she acted older than her age, other times Thessalonike acted with an immaturity that astounded Aya.

They came from different worlds. Aya remembered her homeland every waking moment. She was born within Tyre's walls. Her mother was a body slave and her father was another nameless slave or perhaps a soldier. She had been picked out for her quick and able hands. Her face was unmarred and her short stature gave her an almost constant childlike appearance. The old queen had favored her. She was neither a threat that might catch the king's eye nor was she lazy.

Aya was loyal like a dog. That's what the other slaves had called her when they teased her, but she shrugged off their insults. At least she never got whipped or punished, and her reputation had ensured her survival. While many of the slaves had been mowed down as the Macedonians filled the castle halls, she had been barricaded with the queen in her rooms and was spared a worse fate.

On their journey to Macedonia, she had seen plenty of people consumed by disease, tortured, or even starving, but she had survived. She thanked Isis for looking after such a lowly person. In many ways she was lucky.

It was far better to be attached to a powerful personage than to try to go it alone. That's what life had taught her. It was the free peasants who always seemed to suffer from their supposed freedom. They died by the swords of invaders or were starved by their lord's taxes.

For her at least, it had been better to live in the palace as a servant. Perhaps one day when the world was at peace and the great wars ended, then she too would dream of having a house of her own with a husband and children.

For now, she followed her mistress, grateful for the safety she had and all the little presents she received. Thessalonike was a kind mistress. She always had clean clothes and was given simple jewelry and adornments for her hair. She was dressed better than some of the wives she had seen at banquets back in Tyre.

She was proud of herself and had positioned herself high among the other servants in the royal household. After all, she served the sister of Alexander the Great.

Thessalonike hid her face with her veil in an effort to protect her skin from the remaining sunlight and to keep some of the smells and dirt off her face as well.

The training yard was a part of the man's world that she rarely glimpsed. She spotted other slave girls watching a wrestling match in the center with hungry lustful eyes. She did not join them but stood on the other side of the arena and watched.

She recognized Maro's dark hair immediately. He was wrestling a red-haired man. Both were covered in a sheen of sweat from the effort. She saw they were evenly matched. It was clear from the way neither of them could seem to manage to pin the other down.

There weren't too many people gathered to see these green men fighting, but some were yelling suggestions from the sidelines and egging the men on. Thessalonike did not concern herself too much with what they were saying. She found herself getting caught up in the match.

She shouted with the others when Maro's opponent used a stone to slam into his shoulder, leaving a cut there. It had the desired effect, for Maro stumbled back in shock, releasing his grip on the man's left arm and stomach.

The man then rushed forward and pushed him to the ground. Maro struggled to get him off. Luckily, the man had not been anticipating much of a reaction. He thought he had won and that was when Maro struck his foot out, sweeping behind his opponent. In the next second, he had his opponent pinned to the ground and was holding him by the hair.

Thessalonike shivered at the intensity she saw in his eyes at that moment and looked away when he caught her gaze.

"Do you yield?" he asked, looking down at the man who was now beet red.

The man nodded and Maro released him, helping him to his feet.

They shook hands and parted ways.

Maro wiped the sweat from his face and chugged directly from a pitcher of water.

Thessalonike saw some of the slave girls trying to approach him. She was surprised by the jealousy she felt and stepped forward. She reached him before the others could and sent them a glare that had them scurrying to find someone else to fawn over.

"What, no sarcastic comment from you, Lady?" Maro asked as he poured the rest of the pitcher over his head, washing away some of the sweat and cooling himself off.

"You fought well enough." Thessalonike covered her nose as she got a whiff of him. "But you need a bath. I'm sure those slave girls would love to help you out with that. Maybe even give you a massage." She tempted him to get a reaction out of him and was rewarded by seeing a blush rise to his cheeks. He always blushed so easily.

Once he had walked into her rooms while she was still getting dressed. He had not seen much, but he had turned red and begged her to forgive him. She was not so prudish to care that he had caught a glimpse of her bare back. Perhaps next time she would turn around and make him faint.

Aya would not approve.

"Aya says I am too mean to you. So I've come to apologize. Do you forgive me?"

"Only if you call those slave girls back after you sent them off chasing after Laris."

Now it was Thessalonike's turn to blush, though she hid it better than he had. "They're annoying and I wanted to speak to you first. I shall be going to the theater tonight, and I suppose you shall have to accompany me." She quickly made up an excuse.

He nodded and excused himself.

Thessalonike watched as he headed off for the baths and shrugged. It wasn't that she was jealous, but she hardly enjoyed thinking that he would be running off to be with other women.

He should be at her beck and call.

Aya did not comment as she helped her into a lavender gown for the theater; a dark violet veil and gold girdle completed the outfit. Tonight the theater troupe was putting on a comedy. Luckily, Thessalonike was free to go.

Olympias was poring over her scrolls and dictating her commands to her underlings. Antipater was entertaining commanders and running the soldiers through their drills. She was not needed, so she might as well enjoy herself.

She climbed into the waiting litter and settled on the cushions beside Aya as they left, Maro following on horseback though the journey was short. He always preferred to ride whenever he could.

That was another thing Thessalonike liked about him. He had a way with horses and seemed to enjoy taking care of them. She was certain that a person who was kind to animals was trustworthy. Some days they talked endlessly about the races and conformation of horses. She usually lost her arguments but swore that if her sister Cynane was here, he would be the one losing.

They arrived without much fanfare, but people quickly recognized the livery and word spread that a royal family member was attending tonight. Many people who had come to the theater stared up at her in amazement. Others with envy. She did not waver under the gazes of hundreds of people as she took her seat. She was used to performing herself.

She thought of the actors preparing backstage and thought with jealousy that at least they got to put aside their masks at the end of the day and return to being anonymous. Fame was overrated, she found. Especially when she wished to enjoy a night without making sure she was behaving like the prim and proper princess she was supposed to be.

Olympias was trying to spread the propaganda of Alexander's illustrious lineage with more fervor than ever. This prestige won him men and made his enemies tremble. There could be worse fates.

Aya procured a silk cushion for her to sit on, and she sat back watching the show. Trying not to look at Maro, though she felt as though his gaze was on her. Aya sat beside her looking with interest at the play. She was truly passionate about the comedies and tragedies she witnessed, though she found it amusing that the Greek actors were all male.

She had not thought much of her mistress's actions. She was always tormenting her guard one way or another. The little princess thought she could defend herself instead of being grateful for the protection.

But Aya had failed to notice the way Thessalonike had held her breath when he had been hit by the rock on the training field and how she stole glances at him whenever he wasn't looking.

❦ 3 ❧

Aigai, 331 BC

Thessalonike was anxious for her journey to begin. She paced through the corridors and palace rooms, trying to distract herself. She would be traveling to her mother's old home.

As she was preparing to leave, she had berated Olympias with questions about her.

"What did she look like? Was she fair-skinned or tanned like me?" Thessalonike asked eagerly as she helped oversee the packing of her trunks and chests.

"You take after her with your wavy black hair, but you are taller than she was. You would be fair-skinned too if you were more careful and wore a veil in the sun," Olympias scolded. Thessalonike was now seventeen, and it was time for her to put childish antics aside.

Her journey would take her to Athens to reinforce their power base there.

Alexander agreed with Antipater that the best way to

cement their alliance was with a marriage. Thessalonike was the bait, but Olympias doubted if the betrothal would come to fruition.

This would be the third time Thessalonike had been betrothed to someone.

For her part, Olympias did not mind keeping her youngest child around a bit longer. There was no need to rush and have her married off to some fool.

Now that Athens was grumbling under the yoke of Alexander's rule and Sparta was amassing an army of their own, they could no longer wait. Especially when Darius was at the center of this sudden scheming. He had provided them with ships and funds.

The main Macedonian army was with Alexander moving east. Darius wished to find a way to stall his progress or, even better, ensure that Alexander lost his secure home base.

Perhaps his strategy would have worked had it not been for Antipater and Olympias's political machinations.

Both of them hoped it would not come to war. They were unsure they would be successful and how many of their allies would remain true to them if Athens and Sparta rose against them.

Along with Thessalonike's betrothal, there would be other treaties and agreements to be signed.

The trip she had embarked on was a long one, but it was not for her pleasure. She had a job to do. The secrets and plans Olympias had instructed her in could be recited back without much trouble. Perhaps Thessalonike wasn't the pale beauty that would launch ten thousand ships, but she was smart and that was worth more.

She would not be traveling as just Thessalonike,

daughter of Phillip, king of Macedonia. She would have to embody the otherworldly heritage of her half-brother. She would be a walking representation of his power, and she would have to play her part impeccably well.

It had bolstered her proud nature when Olympias had given her this important task. Usually, she had nothing more important to do than sit up straight and behave herself. Now she would be gathering information and playing the part of the sly politician. It would be up to her to bring Athens to heel—or at least that's what she liked to imagine.

The company of men and women setting out with her was unusually large. With them came a retinue of wagons of gifts and items needed for the long journey. She liked that they had decided to have her travel to Athens by land. A trip over the Aegean Sea would have taken a mere day or two. By land, she would take five days.

Five days in which she would be free to explore the places she had only dreamed of or heard spoken about in stories. She had never left Macedonia, and now she would be exploring all of Greece.

The journey had her stopping at several key sites along the way, not only as a method of propaganda to let the people see her and ignite the people's loyalties to Alexander, but also to bolster her own importance.

Secretly she relished this opportunity. She had pored over the maps the cartographers had drawn up. They would be passing by Mount Olympus, going through Thessaly, visiting the temple at Delphi, and traveling past the ruins of Thebes. She had shivered at that last thought. She wasn't eager to look upon a destroyed city.

Olympias had traveled with her as far as Alexandria at

the edge of Macedonia. The city now shared its name with several other cities from Egypt to India, but it had been Alexander's first conquest and so was special.

Maro had accompanied her as well, but he was not her only protector, though he was the one she trusted the most. Before they had left she had made secret sacrifices of her own to Apollo for protection and to Hermes for speed. She hoped they would not encounter bandits, nor that she would face other misfortunes.

When she had told Aya about her fear of being abducted in the night, Aya had laughed at her. But Aya did not know the Greeks that well yet. Abduction was a very real part of life and myth in Greece. Hoping to remedy her ignorance, Thessalonike had jumped right in retelling all the instances of important heroines being abducted—from Helen of Troy to Kore and Hades.

"Those tales all end in love."

"And disaster," Thessalonike whispered back so Maro wouldn't overhear.

"You are too young for love." Aya patted her head to comfort her.

"I am not a child. I am older than Helen was the first time she was kidnapped."

"So you wish to be kidnapped?"

"No!" Thessalonike snapped back. Her childish impudence still made an appearance every once in a while.

"Is everything all right?" Maro parted the curtains of her litter pulled by two hulking horses after he heard the shout.

"Yes, everything is fine." Thessalonike turned away from him and began fanning herself as though she had not cried out moments ago.

Aya chuckled to herself but did not say another word. Thessalonike did not hate her for her impudence, nor did she have her whipped. In a way, the princess was desperate for a companion. All of her other siblings were much older than she was and had moved away by the time she was ten years old.

She had been brought to prominence by Olympias, but that had not won her much favor with the courtiers in Pella. They kept their children away from her out of caution. So through happenstance Thessalonike had become a stray who was raised by and played with slaves and servants alike.

The horses pulled the litter forward, the wheels bouncing awkwardly as they went over rocks or pot holes in the road.

It wasn't like the gentle swaying she was used to when she was carried in her usual litter from place to place.

On the first day, they had been lucky not to have any trouble with the wheels and the retinue moved smoothly through the countryside. The soldiers guarding her had their eyes peeled on the road ahead of them, looking out for any obstacles or dangers.

She felt safe. The mostly open roads between cities felt devoid of danger. Her experience had led her to believe that it was in the confines of walls and palace rooms that the most danger lay. She thought again of her father, and then Europa's innocent face appeared and she had to blink a few times to rid her mind of the baby's smiling face.

Several noblemen had offered their villas and great houses as a place for her to rest on her journey. Olympias and Antipater had selected them carefully, although in Thessaly she had stayed in her own villa.

Olympias had told her this had been where her mother had stayed in the early years of her marriage to Phillip. He had used it often as a base for his dealings with the other Greek states, and since Alexander was never going to make use of the great manor, she might as well stay there.

🐚

Thessaly, 331 BC

This was the land of her mother. The soft rolling plains. The tilled fertile soil and olive trees.

Maro had thrown her a couple of apricots, ripe and ready to be eaten. They smelled so fragrant that Thessalonike wished she could bathe in their scent and made a note to inquire if such a thing was possible.

In her excitement to see Thessaly and explore her roots, the glory of Mount Olympus almost seemed to be a disappointment.

In fact, she was surprised by how small the mountain seemed. Did the gods really live up there?

Aya was sticking her head through the drapes to get a better look at the home of the gods too. Ever since arriving, Thessalonike had been filling her head with stories and tales of these great gods.

"Are you sure that's Mount Olympus?" she asked Maro, who looked both shocked and insulted by her question.

"It is smaller than you would think," she admitted. "But very majestic and beautiful, to be sure," Thessalonike added in case the gods were listening. She didn't want to be heard insulting their home. That would surely bring bad luck upon her head. Perhaps they might destroy her own home in punishment.

She pulled on Aya's wig, and she jumped back with a yelp before Thessalonike told her to stop blaspheming.

Aya was always so sensitive about her wig.

Now Pharae was before her, and her mind once again fixated on her mother's home and the land of her birth.

The palace was situated near the cliffside. Huts and stone houses sprawled in front of it, and its high walls kept thieves and intruders out relatively well. They were protected by the Peiros River at the back of the palace.

Thessalonike had chosen the room overlooking the inner courtyard with its little fountain. There was a lovely terrace where she sat that night eating her dinner, and she swore she could hear the sound of crashing waves in the distance.

This was more of a villa resort than a proper palace, but the strategic position in Pharae was clear. You could mount an attack from either the river, the nearby sea, or the land while also protecting your back and having access to multiple escape routes if necessary.

Tomorrow night they would throw a great feast for all the noble families to attend. Pollux was overseeing the slaves prepare the palace to Thessalonike's instructions. For the first time in her life, she was now the first lady of the household. She would be playing the part of the hostess and she needed to do it well. Still, it was a daunting task for her considering all the things she had to consider. The menu, the entertainment, procuring decorations, and other things she had not considered.

She had settled on honoring Nike, the goddess of victory, for tomorrow's festivities. Not only was it her namesake, but it would give her the chance to flatter the nobles. She arranged for tableaus to be made of their victories—from the fight with the Persians to expelling the dictator Lycophran to establish the Thessalian League.

She wondered if Olympias would like this nice touch. Their emblems littered the hall, but at the center of the hall where she would be seated was Alexander's standard. Larger than the others, it was a silent reminder that they owed their allegiance to Macedonia.

But for now, she could relax with her maid and lie on couches in the moonlight.

She almost fell asleep before Aya led her inside and she fell on a soft feather bed, sinking into delightful oblivion. Was there any reason for her to leave this place?

She was awoken the next morning by a knock at her door. Aya opened it and allowed the slaves carrying platters of fish, eggs, bread, and oils in for her breakfast.

Thessalonike was not hungry yet, but she picked at the food and exclaimed that it was the best she had ever had. Her words would no doubt travel from the ears of the slaves to those of their masters. People she had to impress.

She was shown to the bath and with Aya attending her prepared herself for the day ahead.

"Do you think we could escape for a bit?" she asked Aya, who thought for a moment.

"You can do what you like as long as it is safe and you don't leave the city."

"I should very much like to go down to the river. The one I can see from my rooms." Thessalonike groaned as the knots in her back were massaged out. Sitting for days at a time had its disadvantages. "It looks like it's just a short ride away. We wouldn't need to leave for more than a few hours. I am sure they can survive without me."

She was talking aloud now.

"And I suppose Maro will insist on accompanying us." She sighed, though she was not entirely annoyed by the thought.

Now that she was dressed in a clean gown and had washed her hair, she summoned Maro to her and they left her rooms, trying not to bring too much attention to themselves. People were running about busily making preparations, but they did not need her. They operated like a well-trained legion—marching to her orders.

They walked past the guards at the entrance of the palace and made their way to the stables. Aya was deathly afraid of horses, so she hung back and watched from afar as her mistress inspected the various creatures.

"This is Zephyrus. I named him after the west wind." She patted a gray gelding's neck. "He is a fast runner but not suited to war. Like you perhaps?"

"You are trying to get a reaction out of me." That wasn't a question.

"I might come to like you. Go see to your horse. Maybe we can leave Aya behind. She hates horses and would rather be dismissed from accompanying me."

"I don't trust you with this scoundrel," Aya called out. "I'll come with you."

"I can carry her," Maro interjected.

"All right." Thessalonike was anxious to get going now.

His bay mare was well-built and looked as strong as any of the other horses in the stable.

Aya had agreed to ride pillion behind Maro and held on

tight to him as the horses ran out of the stables, kicking up dust as they went.

Thessalonike led her horse down the trail to the river. She hated swimming, but the sound of this gentle river and the breeze relaxed her.

"You have a wonderful horse," Maro complimented her when they had reached the beach and led the horses by their reins through the sand.

"My sister Cynane sent him and another to me as betrothal gifts." She laughed, remembering the irritated letter from her when her last betrothal was broken. It had read: *I can't afford to keep this up*. She had been joking of course, but Thessalonike had assured her she did not need more horses.

Sitting on a rock, she watched from afar as Aya walked into the water ankle deep. She soaked in the chilling breeze, enjoying the way it blew past her face and cooled her down.

Eventually, they had to return. She could not stay out all day like some lowborn woman.

As she bathed and was dressed by her maids, Maro waited outside her rooms. He played the part of the unmovable guard quite well, but she preferred it when she was teasing him. He thought that she didn't notice the way he would sometimes glare at her, but that had not been the case.

She found his antics amusing.

"Do you think I'll be in great danger tonight? You are free to enjoy yourself. There are plenty of guards to watch out for me here." They were in her room now and she was plucking at her lyre, waiting for time to pass.

He bowed but did not say what he would do, and Thessalonike dismissed him.

After her lunch, she had taken another bath. Her hair had been curled and another maid had helped Aya arrange her dark hair into a crown on her head. Not a hair was to be out of place. She had picked a pale blue himation gown to wear for tonight's feast. Silver necklaces and sapphire pendants clashed with her dark hair and matched the gown. She was trying to inspire an image of wealth and power.

Back in Pella, she would only wear such luxuries on special occasions, but now she would be draped in gold and jewels constantly. Olympias had been adamant about her paying attention to her image.

The Greek city-states were different from Macedonia. Despite being able to conquer all of Greece, it was still considered an uncouth place without etiquette.

Thessalonike had learned long ago that each place or people had its own culture, and you could not force people to conform to your ideas. It was far better and easier to adapt.

Aya was dressed in a clean white gown as well with a blue sash as a girdle to match her mistress. She would be attending to her personally.

As the guests arrived, Thessalonike sent her out to report on who had come and how they behaved or seemed to act.

"Nothing out of the ordinary. Some complained about the musty smell in the dining room."

Thessalonike rolled her eyes. There was no smell, but of course they would be implying that the absence of the royal family had allowed this house to fall into disuse and ruin. "What are they wearing?"

"Their best jewels and clothes. I could tell because of the way they are so careful to avoid spilling wine or food passed out by the servants."

Thessalonike grinned. "Well, it should be time for my grand entrance soon."

Her entrance went off without an issue, and it definitely caught their eyes. Two guards on either side flanked her as she entered to the sounds of musicians playing. She remained stoic as she faced off with many old politicians and aristocrats. She did not wish to give them the chance to look down upon her. She wanted to seem larger than life, and for now it seemed as though she had accomplished that.

Tonight's festivities would go smoothly if she had anything to say about it.

She finally reached the dais and took a seat beside the makeshift throne representing Alexander.

The mayor of Pharae stepped forward and gave a quick little speech, going on about the honor she was bestowing upon the city with her visit. He spoke of unflinching loyalty to her family and of the love the people held in their hearts for Alexander.

He was exaggerating—even Thessalonike knew that—but she smiled and rewarded him with a small purse of coins for his kind words.

Tonight awards and gifts would be doled out with enthusiasm. The cost was nothing in comparison to the treasure Alexander was sending back to Macedonia, and it was cheaper to ensure loyalty through little gifts than to try to subjugate them by force.

Honey, not vinegar, would win here tonight.

It was not long before dancers and acrobats appeared out of hidden alcoves. The guests took their seats and began eating, drinking, and talking.

At the center of it all was Thessalonike. It was uncommon for a woman to be center stage—the Greeks preferred their women silent and obedient. However, Thessalonike was a princess too, and she would have to gain their favor one way or another. If all she could do was throw lavish parties for them, then she would make do.

If they spoke out of turn, not fearing the power she held, that would be fine too. She would store and collect all the information she could. So let them underestimate her influence.

She was enjoying a cup of warmed wine now that the evening had cooled the room significantly. The sea breeze ensured that braziers were needed most nights, even in the summer, but it was refreshing.

Most of the entertainments had finished. As she had predicted, most of her guests had been flattered to see the victories of their forefathers and their own played out in front of them. Enticing them with wine had helped as well. All the while she remained alert and attentive.

Some men had begun reminiscing about the old days when Phillip had arrived with his armies and conquered Greece.

Someone had responded that the wars were still going on—draining away all the young men.

Some laughed, saying they did not mind ridding themselves of ambitious men trying to make a fortune. "Let them go off and stop bothering us," a man shouted.

"You only say that, Alcides, because you have seven

sons and all of them are hungry wolves," a man who was quite drunk shouted in response.

This made the men laugh, even the man who had been insulted. "That is very true! The gods gave me a double-edged sword. On one hand I have more heirs than I need, on the other, I don't know how I am to choose which should inherit."

"Have them compete in the games, and see which is the best."

Thessalonike hid a grin by taking another gulp of wine. Most families did not have this problem and it was amusing to make light of the situation, but she also understood the downsides of this.

With so many hungry mouths there would not be enough money and land to satisfy them all. No wonder this father encouraged his sons to try to make their fortunes with Alexander and his army. He rewarded those soldiers who fought well with land, and he was generous when it came to sharing the booty they collected.

After the laughter had stopped, another man decided to chime in with something about how those who left were abandoning their Greek heritage.

Thessalonike's hawk-like eyes focused on the man instantly. He had said nothing rude outright, but he was treading on dangerous ground. His words were innocent enough, but his implications, if they were read into too much, were dangerous.

Was he accusing Alexander of no longer being a Greek? Thessalonike knew he had been too focused on personal ambition and vendettas. He no longer lived in Greece like a true king should. Instead, he left the ruling of his kingdom to his advisors and, as some liked to snigger, his mother.

"I have never had such a pleasant evening," Thessalonike interjected, breaking the direction this conversation was going in. "Shall we have some more music? I have heard stories you have some of the best musicians here from all over Greece."

The room nodded and agreed with her.

Musicians appeared again, and they enjoyed a ballad.

By the time the night was over, Thessalonike was exhausted. She had to keep alert the whole night, though it was hard to pinpoint everything that was said or done, but the people of Thessaly had welcomed her well enough. She did not think there was much danger.

As she changed into a sleeping robe, she called for Maro on a whim. Aya was busy putting away her jewelry and preparing the gown for tomorrow when he appeared.

"Yes, Lady?" He bowed and waited to hear what she wanted.

Thessalonike wasn't sure how to begin her question. Could she trust him? She looked into his honest brown eyes and thought that here was a loyal man.

"Have you heard anything in the barracks? Any discontentment or words against me or my brother?"

"Nothing outside of the usual complaints. They do question why he has not yet married and produced an heir. They think the dynasty is in danger of dying with him."

"I wonder if they think that is a good thing," she thought aloud. He looked taken aback by her statement and she gave him a little smile. "I meant nothing by it. Why don't you be my little spy and report to me anything you hear? They are likely to trust you more than me. I know how people can hide their true sentiments. Help me to discover them?"

He licked his lips, suddenly finding them dry. "As you wish, Lady." He bowed again and she dismissed him with a wave of her hand.

Aya came over to her and offered her own assistance too. "The slave quarters are full of gossip too. I shall see if I can find out anything."

Thessalonike nodded. She wanted to get a full picture for when she reported back to Olympias.

On the third morning, Thessalonike bid farewell to the mayor and other citizens who had come to see her off. They wished her luck and hoped she would return someday soon.

The promises and compliments felt as empty and hollow as Aphrodite's beauty. They did not wish to be ruled but rather left alone to manage their own affairs. Thessalonike knew that, but she plastered a smile on her face and did not change her expression until the curtains around her carriage had been drawn closed.

She found she enjoyed traveling, though she could have done without the political intrigue. This was the first time in her whole life that she had ever left Macedonia—would the opportunity to leave ever present itself again?

The sham of this betrothal amused her too.

She wondered how many times it would take before a betrothal would turn into marriage, not that she was in any rush to get married.

She also scolded herself for her pessimism. She was too young to be cynical and it wasn't flattering.

That afternoon Thessalonike, who was getting increasingly hot and bored with sitting down all day, begged Maro to see if he could get the commander of their retinue to agree to stop for lunch. They were not supposed to stop for some time when a small retinue would break off and allow Thessalonike to travel faster to pay her respects at the sacred temple in Delphi.

Still, she was a princess and the highest-ranking person in this little band, even if she was just a girl as Maro liked to remind her, to which she would threaten to have him whipped for insulting her.

Eventually, she got what she wanted. They called a halt to the procession and had the horses watered while Thessalonike strolled beyond the men and their horses, followed by Aya at her side. She wanted to sit underneath the grove trees and feel the breeze on her face as she ate candied apricots and smoked fish with figs. Maro and another guard noticed her wandering away and followed after her.

They shouldn't have been in any danger here, but there was always the risk. Maro would have scolded her for wandering off but didn't know how she would react, so he took his post quietly and without much protest, though he had caught her smiling at him.

When he asked her if she required anything, she only shook her head and leaned back against the tree. She did not mind the bark pressing into her skin or the little bugs that swarmed around them. Anything was welcomed after being in the litter for two days. The motion was getting to her too.

Another servant came over and inquired if they would like entertainment and a flute player materialized, though the captain warned they would need to set out soon.

She could live here. Thessalonike decided to let the music drift her away to another world of pleasant dreams.

Just as she had begun falling asleep, a piercing scream sharply pulled her back.

She was alert and ready, her wide eyes searching for danger left and right.

"What is it?" she hissed to Aya, who lifted a shaky arm to point to the other soldier who was standing under a tree farther away. He had gone to relieve himself when a snake had fallen on him from the trees. It was wrapping itself around his warm neck and he was struggling to remain calm.

Maro was already walking toward the man, a dagger in his right hand.

Thessalonike was on her feet in a flash and, pushing past Maro, urged him to let her handle this with a motion of her hand. He froze in his place and watched.

She quickly identified the snake from the bands. It was poisonous but a gentle sleeping snake that preferred eating bird eggs and chicks to killing people. Ignoring the quaking soldier, she fixated her attention on the snake, whispering to it the lulling spells Olympias had taught her. It was distracted from arranging itself on its new unwilling perch and regarded her with its beady black eyes, flicking its tongue at her.

She continued speaking as she began uncoiling the snake carefully, starting from the tail.

She was finished within seconds and released it to go slithering back to its home. The hot summer sun had made it complacent.

The soldier looked as though he would faint, and Maro

was by his side. "You are fine," he said in a voice that brooked no argument.

"What magic was that?" the soldier asked.

"Not magic." Thessalonike shook her head, though she wished it was. "Snake charming. Besides, you were lucky. That was one of the nicest poisonous snakes I've ever met."

"Poisonous?" The soldier had gone white. It was so strange to see men quaking. They liked portraying themselves as fearless warriors, but Thessalonike knew enough of the world to know the truth.

"I would have dealt with it," Maro said after he sent the soldier to go back to the caravan and get a cup of wine. He would recover his spirits in no time. "You should not have endangered yourself. I am meant to protect you."

"You shouldn't scold me. If you had come at the snake with the knife, you would have frightened it and it would have attacked faster than you could have struck its head off."

He looked unsure but eventually relented. "I shall concede to you on this issue. But don't put yourself in danger like that."

"Or you'll never get promoted with a dead princess on your hands?" She bit her lip, but the words had escaped. Quickly, she retreated within herself again and stored away her worries and concerns.

"Forget what I said," she ordered and went forward without looking at him again. He was left following her with a quizzical look on his face. Usually, she liked to tease him about his desire to get promoted and swore that he never would.

This had been different.

He had been genuinely concerned about her well-being as a living breathing person, but she had immediately jumped to thinking that all he cared about was his career. She was not a means to an end. Not to him. He tried clearing his mind but tucked away this new piece of information he had learned about her.

Thessalonike climbed into the litter and sat on the cushions, suddenly tired and wishing nothing more than to sleep the day away.

Aya had climbed in not long after—she sat across from her mistress with a questioning look on her face, but she did not speak. Now was not the time to bring up why she seemed to be in such a sour mood.

Aya had other concerns to voice too. The event with the snake was sure to send the men talking—she needed to protect her mistress from rumors of the sort. For now, she had remained untainted by association with Olympias, but it wouldn't take long for people to draw conclusions if this story got out.

As she got water, she had heard a man claim that he had heard Thessalonike had talked to the snake and ordered it to go away with magic. This would have to be nipped in the bud quickly. They were traveling through the countryside, but the first of the great cities was not too far away. Word would spread and it could spell disaster.

She could just imagine how people would love to claim that Alexander's women were all sorceresses and that they had to turn against him to free the people from the witchcraft of conniving women.

She had heard it happen before—most of the time the events were completely fabricated too. People in power never tended to stay there for too long. That's what she had noticed. She thought back to Tyre and the several rising and falling stars she had seen.

Eventually, Thessalonike seemed to relax. Whatever she had meditated on had helped clear the cloud that seemed to hang over her head.

Aya knew plenty of women who could never escape the dark thoughts that lingered in everyone's mind. Eventually, that darkness would grow and envelop them. Thessalonike was stronger; she could banish the darkness.

"Mistress, you must think of a way to silence the guards. There is talk of magic happening in that tree grove. The snake was unlucky."

"I saved a man." She was exasperated but did not miss the formal way with which Aya had addressed her. Unless they were in company or at events, she never addressed her like that unless it was important. She had to play the part of the strategist and relinquish the role of the woman.

"They think it is magic."

Thessalonike bit her lip for the second time that day. Gods, it was hot. "I shall think of something. The fool couldn't have kept his mouth shut, could he? Why do all men think that any woman who can do anything useful must be using some dark art?"

Aya smiled a little at the biting comment and hoped no one had heard. "I can massage your temple if your head hurts."

"Would you fan me? I think the heat is getting to me."

Without another word, Aya picked up the peacock fan and set to work. There was no silence for them to relax in. The retinue was loud as it progressed at its slow lumbering pace. Even though they did not speak, they heard plenty of conversations going on around them, though sometimes it was hard to pick out the words.

By the time they had reached the fork in the road, the company settled down to rest for a few hours. They would head to Thessaly and make it there before it got too late, but for now a smaller retinue was splitting off and would be escorting Thessalonike to the Temple of Delphi, where she would pray and pay for an offering.

As a horse was saddled for her, she held its reins and petted its velvet nose, comforting the creature. Maro pulled up beside her on a horse of his own. "Don't run away from us," he warned her under his breath, and she promised to behave.

They set out at a trot. Few provisions were brought with them, but Thessalonike had given Maro a purse of gold to give to the priests for the sacrifice. Perhaps the oracle would read her future for her or that of her brother's.

As they rode, the men who had at first been uneasy in her presence relaxed as she spoke joyfully of horses and all that she knew about them. She was no stranger to worming her way into the hearts of her companions.

Now she set about charming them.

As the men began joking, she joined in with a story of her own.

"I heard Proxis has made up quite the tale with me and a snake."

The men quieted for a moment but leaned forward in their saddles to hear what she had to say.

"He had gone off and a little garden snake had fallen on him. He gave such a scream that Maro pulled his knife. Proxis was so frozen in fear that I took pity on him and got rid of the snake. I just pushed it off him, but I thought I'd punish him for squealing like a girl." The men laughed. "I whispered to him that it was a poisonous snake. Of course, I was referring to his fear, for with such a weak heart how will he ever fight properly in a war? Anyway, that was probably cruel of me. I shall have to ask his forgiveness."

Maro had not said anything at the beginning but was surprised by her simplistic and neat solution to a potentially dangerous rumor.

He did not exaggerate nor did he deny her story. He simply laughed along with the others, nodding here and there. The men lapped it up. The comedic scene was much more believable than magic. Especially from such an innocent-looking lady who rode horses so well and did not need to hold on to someone.

They worshiped Alexander, even though it had been years since they had seen him in person, but they were loyal to the idea he represented. Here was his sister, who seemed to be down to earth but also just out of reach.

She could ride like them but dressed in fine silks like a proper lady. She did not squeal at harmless snakes, but neither did she carry a sword and spear like an amazon. She seemed to them a genial lady with just the right amount of pluck and feminine wiles.

The country was still divided on her eldest sister Cynane, who was a warrior through and through, having finally accomplished her goal to lead men into battle.

Maro, who had been with her long enough to know how she worked, was surprised by the effect she seemed to have on the men. With surprising ease, she seemed to win their trust.

The ride was over quicker than he could have imagined. The white columns and the marble dome gleamed in the sun up ahead as they rode up the cobbled road. They weren't the only people making their way to the temple, but they were the most important. The crowds parted for them as one of the soldiers bearing the standard of Alexander's royal family was recognized.

They looked at Thessalonike with renewed interest. Was she a sister? Cousin?

The city of Delphi was prosperous despite having been raided during her father's reign. They marched past the Sibyl rock and the treasury, beyond which Thessalonike caught a glimpse of the terrace of the Temple of Apollo. That was their destination.

A bald priest greeted them at the temple steps.

They were ushered in and allowed into the cella of the temple. Thessalonike tipped them generously, already knowing what was expected of her, and said a prayer before the statue of Apollo.

From there she was taken to the front of the temple where the altar was waiting, directly positioned in the line of sight of the statue inside. The head priest introduced himself and asked her what business she had here today.

"I wish to pay tribute to Apollo and make a sacrifice to him to send my brother Alexander victory and favor." She struggled to keep from gaping at the beautiful temple. A statue of the goddess Nike running crowned the temple. It was unimaginable how such a stunning structure could be built. Inside she had seen colorful frescoes despite the dim light. Outside she got a better look at the temple and saw that each of the roof tiles was decorated with images of sphinxes, griffins, and other mythical beings.

"Your wish is our command." He bowed and, raising his hand, he flicked forward a few of the priests waiting in the alcoves.

They began chanting and a white bull was brought out. This would be a great sacrifice indeed. Olympias had planned this out a few weeks ago—the bowing, the bull, and the grand gesture that would follow. A crowd had gathered to watch what the priests would say.

The bull was sacrificed, and when they spilled its entrails a shock went up from the crowd as the cow's liver was pulled out. It was golden.

"The Sun God shines upon his son and brother. Alexander, king of Macedonia, emperor of the Persians, and conqueror of the world, will never be stopped," the high priest intoned as he stared at the liver.

The crowd gasped, muttering among themselves. Never before had they heard of such a sign.

Thessalonike fell to her knees as delicately as she could and in a loud voice thanked Apollo and all the gods for the favor bestowed on her family. Saying they were the lowliest of servants wishing to unite the world under one banner for the honor of the gods.

This was her special touch. It had all been planned out well in advance. The liver covered in gold leaf was nothing more than a substitute. They had paid copious amounts of coin for this favorable reading. Perhaps it was asking for trouble bribing a priest to read something in the entrails, but it was all in a day's work.

The gods would understand. People needed to know of Alexander's divinity. They needed to be assured that all who stood in his way would perish by his sword.

From her belt Thessalonike pulled out an additional

generous purse and laid it in the hands of a waiting priest, who scurried away with it.

They drank some water and ate bread dipped in olive oil and were once again heading down the path to rejoin the rest of their retinue.

They moved at a slower pace until they were farther away from the temple in an effort to appear modest and taken aback by the majesty of the event that had taken place. But time was of the essence, and Thessalonike was not a zealot. Out of sight, they urged their horses forward at a gallop.

"That was well done." Maro congratulated her in hushed tones when they had separated from the rest of the guards.

"I didn't do much. It was the priests who did all the dirty work." She shrugged.

"No, I was talking about convincing the others about what had happened earlier with the snake. I am sure the incident will be forgotten about and laughed at instead of whispered about in corners."

"Ah, yes. Well, it's ridiculous this even had to be dealt with." She rolled her eyes. She was annoyed that an incident like this could stain her reputation.

They were back on the road within an hour of their return. Aya was curious about what had happened at the temple, but there was not much to tell her. Besides the beautiful temple, nothing noteworthy had happened, nor had she had time to explore properly.

❊ 4 ❊

Athens, 331 BC

Their journey took them past the ruins of Thebes. The once great city looked as though it was still in shambles. Its once great walls had been torn down. There were still charred marks on the buildings and stones from when Alexander had ordered the city burned to the ground.

On the outskirts of the city, people had rebuilt, and she was sure in time the city too would be rebuilt as much as possible. But for now, they avoided the ruins, both in fear of Alexander's wrath and the ghosts of the people killed there.

At first, she had been tempted to stop and walk the streets of the ruined city. She had never seen such destruction before, but she had changed her mind when the time came and they whizzed by the ruins without another look.

Besides, her entourage was nervous that they might encounter problems.

Maro had mentioned it lightly, but she knew what it meant. More than a few people in the area had a bone to pick with Alexander and what he had done to their homes and families. Most people had been enslaved, but some had gotten away.

She couldn't blame people for wanting to seek revenge too.

Finally, their long journey seemed to be at an end. As they approached Athens, she snuck a look at the approaching city. The first thing she noticed was the Parthenon perched on top of the central hill of the city. Even from a distance, she could see the marvelous Acropolis littered with temples and other important buildings. She would make an effort to see it in person. This had been a masterpiece built only several years ago. A temple dedicated to Athena.

The city itself was enormous, but unlike other cities, there were no huge siege walls or a standing army. This was the commercial and cultural epicenter of all of Greece. They had once been a military power to contend with too, but this was no longer the case.

Instead, Athens had become fixated on the arts and sciences. She looked at the statues as they entered the city. Their white marble shone in the sunlight, blinding her for a moment.

She sat back away from the curtains. She did not want people seeing her act like an errant child sneaking a peak.

Their retinue was led through the busy city streets at a lumbering pace. As a visiting foreign dignitary and sister to Alexander the Great, she was an oddity and people had come out to try to catch a glimpse of her.

She was dressed in a yellow gown today, but after five

hours of travel, she hardly looked majestic or imperial. They'd be disappointed if they saw her.

Finally, they pulled into the walled gates of a palace and the curtains of her carriage were pulled back.

Three men greeted her—the strategoi of Athens. One of them, Phocion, would be her father-in-law. She regarded him for a moment longer. She had heard a lot about him. Besides standing up to her father, he also openly argued with Alexander and wrote lengthy messages and speeches preaching against his tactics. He was at least a head taller than her and although old age had left him with a face covered in wrinkles, he seemed no less intelligent and quick of mind. His bright blue eyes studied her just as much as she had done to him.

Then the introductions were over and she was shown to her rooms. Her retinue would be housed nearby or in the palace, and her horses and animals would be tended to.

She did not have time to fully prepare for dinner, but she did her best to clean herself. Aya brushed her tangled hair with a comb and struggled to style it neatly.

Antipater's representative would be speaking to the senate and trying to finalize a final treaty. At the end of the week, the betrothal ceremony would take place, but in the meantime she could do her own recon between the events she was asked to attend and taking a tour of the city.

She would be charming allies for Macedonia, while also trying to determine whether or not they would betray them.

The next day she was officially introduced to her betrothed, Phocus. He was twenty-five years old and had a genial look about him. He was pleasant enough to her but just as disinterested as well.

He asked about her journey and promised to give her a tour of the city—with an appropriate escort of course. He added this quickly, as though he worried about offending her sensibilities.

What Thessalonike was most interested in hearing about was his time in Sparta. According to rumors, when he had reached his majority he had become quite wild, shaming his illustrious father. In response, Phocion had sent him to Sparta to be trained and raised as a proper Greek. He had hoped to rid his son of his excesses. She wondered if he had indeed been tamed. He definitely had a hardened look about him and old scars covered his arms. Those he probably gained on the training yard in Sparta, where they were renowned for their harsh training tactics.

There was another reason she was so curious.

Phocion claimed they did not side with Sparta and that both city-states kept out of each other's hair on principle. How could this be true when he had trusted them enough with his only son?

She put thoughts of intrigue aside as she was shown to the room where the wives of the important men and women had gathered to host a little party for her. She would be introduced and they would act as her chaperones in the absence of Olympias.

As they greeted her, she could not help but think that they reminded her of cobras circling her, testing her for weakness. She squared her back and lifted her head to meet their gazes, undaunted while trying to give the illusion of calmness.

Demetria came forth. She was Phocion's second wife, and the rumors of her austerity proved to be correct. She was dressed in an elegant but plain white robe. Her hair was neatly tied back in a bun and only a plain gold pendant hung at her neck. Yet for all her plainness, she was the one in charge here.

In fact, as Thessalonike looked around, the other women were trying to emulate this important woman. They all wore muted colors and seemed to wear as little adornment as possible. Thessalonike felt overdressed but did not let it bother her.

She returned the woman's greeting with sincerity and let her lead her around the hall introducing her to the other women. However, as soon as she learned their names she seemed to forget them just as quickly. She did not plan to be here too long, but Demetria seemed certain of the forthcoming marriage to her stepson. She talked at length about Athens and the great honor it would be for her to come live here.

The elder woman was trying to be kind as she pointed out etiquette and behaviors that Thessalonike should remember in the future. For example, she should always wear a veil in the presence of a man.

"When you travel you should not go about unveiled. It is unseemly to do so. It would make people think you are a common woman."

Thessalonike smiled. A darkness fell over her face at the barely concealed insult. "I am the sister of the conqueror of the world. I can do as I please. No one would mistake me for a common woman."

Demetria was too polite to scold her, so she nodded and agreed. "Of course, I just wished to tell you how things are done in Athens. After all, you might be marrying my stepson, and you would be moving from the court of your illustrious brother to Athens. But there is plenty of time for you to accustom yourself. I know how hard it must have been to grow up without a mother. We hear such rumors about the wildness of Macedonia I can scarcely believe them." Which meant to say that she did.

"I am sure they are exaggerated." Thessalonike grabbed a piece of sugared dates rolled in pistachios as though she did not care about the insults thrown her way. The woman might be known for her austerity, but she could cut as deeply as any other.

"Tell me about my betrothed. I hear he was sent to Sparta to train. Now that is a wild, tough place. Fit only for beasts, or so I hear."

Demetria forced a smile. "He was sent to the very best warriors to learn to lead an army, and he fought with the best. He went as a boy and returned a man. These are not things you should concern yourself with. He has the very best disposition."

The other women twittered around them, affirming her claims.

Thessalonike pressed on. "Surely the Spartans cannot be better than the Macedonian cavalry? You should have sent him to us."

Demetria did not answer for a moment. Probably thinking about what she should say. "Of course, the Macedonians are legendary in their military expeditions. I did not mean to insult you in any way." Then she changed the topic, asking what Thessalonike liked to do in her spare time.

She answered the questions with prepared answers as her mind churned over this piece of information. Clearly, there was still some camaraderie between the Spartans and the Athenians. Were the Athenians really prepared to stand against their neighbors? They did not seem to have much regard for Alexander or Macedonia, for that matter.

But what did these women know? They had never seen Macedonia and merely resented its power.

Already, Thessalonike wished to return home.

She discovered it was difficult to find any time alone. After a while, she wondered if this had not been done on purpose. They wanted to keep her busy and make sure someone was always watching her. Did they think she was a passive fool that wouldn't notice? Perhaps they did.

It would not be the first time someone had underestimated her.

The next time she saw Phocus at a dinner party she approached her betrothed full of excitement and guile.

"I heard such wonderful tales from my slave about the Athenian warriors and ships. I cannot believe the stories that sprang from her mouth. She said some warriors battle in the arena with lions and that you have ships that can skim across the water. Is it true? I wouldn't trust anyone else." She pouted her lips as though she was terribly confused.

He obliged her by assuring her the Athenians had strong and able soldiers. He went on to describe their various exploits—most of these stories she knew were exaggerated, but she hung on to his every word and he seemed to enjoy that. He also let it slip that Athens did not have much of a standing army but called upon volunteers and conscripted men from the countryside. This was not news, but the specific number of the army seemed small to her. Still, she gasped as though she thought that was a large army. He laughed at her and told her their army had been far greater in the past.

"But now is a time for peace, is it not?" His hand brushed hers as he moved closer to her while they walked about the room. Giggling at his hidden meaning, she hid what he imagined was a blush behind her fan and looked away. By playing the doting fool she seemed to have sparked some interest in him now.

"Tell me more about Athens. Is it true the ships sail so smoothly that you neither rock nor stumble on the deck?"

"It is true. Would you like to see them?" he asked, and she caught him staring at her with a heated gaze. His eyes not on her face but focused lower. She cringed, disgusted at the man for being so obvious, but kept her opinions to herself.

"I would love to. Besides, it might be cooler by the sea."

"I promise to arrange it soon," he promised her, and she rewarded him by giving his hand a little squeeze.

She supposed she was acting like a shameless flirt all afternoon because she caught Maro's exasperated expression as he stood guard. It wasn't necessary for him to attend—they were surrounded by guards and the busy pavilions were hardly the place for any real danger. But every morning he had appeared outside her doors, waiting to follow her wherever she went.

"I promised your mother that I would watch you."

"I am not a child." She rolled her eyes but did not complain much. Thessalonike did not really mind his presence anymore.

In the end, plans were finalized to go to the docks tomorrow, and the outing would give her an opportunity to wander around without raising suspicion. She would see if they truly did have such fantastic ships and how many too.

They could be a real threat if they decided to support Sparta.

That evening, after the slaves had cleaned up her room for the night and had been dismissed, Thessalonike called for Aya and they whispered like old friends. She confided in her how she loathed Phocus, though he seemed to go out of his way to please her. There was another thing that irked her.

"Am I being watched?"

"What do you mean?" Aya whispered back, her eyes glinting from the light of the one remaining lamp that was burning low.

"I feel as though I am being herded. I am dragged from one party to another—no one talks to me about anything important. I suppose Antipater's man is having better luck in the senate, but I wonder if they are trying to hide something from me," she mused as quietly as she could.

Aya shrugged. "I haven't heard much, but no one would talk about it with me anyway. However, I doubt they think it is your place to talk politics. You are a visiting princess, not a royal dignitary," she reminded her mistress gently. In her head, she added that she was a woman—of course no one would let her wander around.

"Well, I shall have to plot my escape one night. I'll ask Maro to help."

"Promise me you won't. It would be too dangerous." Aya grabbed her hand.

"You worry too much. I am tired now. Thank you for listening to me, and remember to try to keep an ear out and your eyes peeled for news."

Aya nodded and left to go sleep on her little couch outside her rooms. She would stand guard in her own little way and be nearby if there were any problems. Besides, the palace was overcrowded with visitors and there was hardly a free place to sleep. The steward of the house had been more than willing to let her sleep by the door, though it might not have seemed dignified.

Maro could not sleep that night. All he could think of was Thessalonike pawing at that man for attention. He had never seen her act this way, and for some reason it disturbed him. Perhaps she had truly come to love this man, but he couldn't believe it.

He had always seen her as a little annoying sister, until this afternoon when she had emerged from her rooms in a new gown that showed more of her bare shoulders than usual and a gold collar that brought attention to her elegant neck. She looked more like a grown woman than the girl he had seen running to pet her horse in the stables.

He had convinced himself that these thoughts were nothing more than innocent observations. Only a blind man could claim ignorance. As for his annoyance, he was here to protect her, and of course he distrusted the Athenian man she would soon be engaged to. She was the sister of the man he idolized, he was staunchly devoted to her and any other of Alexander's kin. That was all.

In the end, he allowed himself to get pulled away by fellow soldiers to the wine shops and taverns to drink the night away and enjoy themselves for once.

The smell of stale beer, spilled wine, and other unmentionables assaulted his nose as he stepped inside. It was likely that he had spent too much time in fine houses. His upbringing had been grand enough, but he was not a snob.

They found an empty table and ordered their drinks. Eventually, the usual customers forgot about the newcomers. Indeed, many of his fellow officers had become quite drunk, run off with bar wenches, or returned home.

Maro found himself drinking alone at the table and contented himself with his drink. He decided he would leave as soon as he had finished one last cup, when he heard the name Alexander mentioned by a particularly drunk man.

His mind fought to clear the haze of the drink, and he tried to focus on what the man was saying. He struggled to do so but finally was rewarded for his efforts.

"...off conquering Asia, leaving ripe pickings for us... money to be had for joining...they are paying the men double their usual wages."

The snippets of the conversation he heard were enough to send shivers down his spine. The man might not be an Athenian, of course. He could be a visiting Spartan recruiting soldiers in tavern houses. Maro nearly choked on his drink. That would have been a great idea for a comedy. The Spartans, renowned for training their boys from a very young age to fight and being famously picky with who they let into their ranks, hiring drunk men in a tavern.

He wished to stay longer to hear what the man and his companions had to say and ordered another drink so he wouldn't look suspicious. His efforts did not yield any more information, but he thought with a satisfied smirk that he had found something for Thessalonike.

She surely had to know about this.

He tipped the bartender and left the tavern to make his way back home. He must have been stumbling or swaying because a pickpocket tried to come at him, but he was not so drunk that he could not react. His training defended him against the onslaught, and the thief was lying facedown in the streets when he walked past him.

People tended to underestimate him. He was not as big as some of the others, but he had been well trained and was quick on his feet. Fast reflexes could beat brute strength if used correctly.

Finally reaching his rooms, he collapsed on his pallet and drifted off to sleep immediately.

He awoke late in the day and jumped to his feet, hoping that Thessalonike had not been pulled away from her rooms just yet. He got dressed, and after checking his sword he sheathed it at his waist.

He nearly broke into a run in anxiety, but he earned himself a few stares and he slowed down to stop drawing so much attention.

Maro met Aya in the hallway carrying a new dress that needed to be mended for Thessalonike.

"You smell of beer." She scrunched her nose up at him. "She is still in her rooms getting ready, so you won't have far to go, but perhaps you should take a bath first."

"There's no time," he muttered. "I must speak to her. It's important."

"The impertinence." But she frowned when she saw his serious face.

"I'll come too. The mending can wait for now."

Thessalonike was strumming a tune on her lyre when she was interrupted by her two loyal companions striding into her room.

This was peculiar.

"What is it?" She looked at both of them, worried for a moment.

"It's nothing serious." Maro stepped forward after Aya elbowed him to hurry up.

"I was in the tavern last night." He paused and looked around. "Will we be overheard?"

Thessalonike was intrigued now. She wasn't positive there wouldn't be someone listening in on them, but she sent Aya to wait by the door and she picked up her lyre and began tuning it. She motioned for Maro to approach and speak quickly.

If anyone entered the room, they would not find anything out of the ordinary, nor was it likely they would have made out what he was whispering over the strums.

He finished speaking, leaving her gaping like a fish. She shut her mouth quickly and urged him to lean close to her. "You must take me there so I can see with my own eyes."

"It would be impossible."

"I'll find a way. I'll send Aya to speak with you. That won't be seen as too suspicious."

He nodded and stepped away. He was tired; the drinking from last night had done a number on him.

Now that the adrenaline had seemed to wear off, he found he needed to sleep more, but he had his duties and would have to force himself to be attentive.

Thessalonike set aside her lyre and paced the room, biting her cheek. She tried to keep the fear from bubbling up and overwhelming her. She was not ready to give in, nor could she let it rule her heart. She couldn't be sure anyway. Maro may have misheard. He had been drunk after all, and who knew what the man had been talking about.

As promised, Phocus took her to sit in one of the famous Athenian ships. She was quick with her compliments and made sure he didn't notice her making a silent count of all the ships at the dock. There were more than there might be usually, but this could just be a busy day—it was hard to tell and she doubted she would have another chance.

She was looking over the edge at the blue water lapping at the side of the boat. It was true the vessel barely moved. It seemed to float on top of the water rather than cutting through it.

"Lady, Phocus is looking for you." Maro had approached.

"Let him look." She grinned and laughed to see a smile on his face. Then she turned her thoughts to more serious matters. "Maro, you must take me to that wine shop again. I want to hear the people for myself."

"You don't trust me?"

"I trust you, but others might not." She shrugged and he knew she was referring to Antipater and Olympias.

"It won't be safe for you to go, and if you come with guards..."

"It'll be perfectly safe. I'll dress like any normal citizen and you will accompany me. It will be simple. No one will notice a soldier and his mistress drinking wine in a shop."

His eyes widened at her words. "My lady, that..."

"Let them think what they want. It doesn't have to be true—we can slip in unnoticed and spy all we like. I'll send Aya to speak to you. It will be at night once everyone has gone to sleep."

"There will always be guards and slaves who remain awake."

"Yes, but the important people will be asleep."

He fixed her with a stare that told her she had been saying stupid things.

"I only mean that they are less likely to remember or report anything, and it will be easier to get away if they assume I am tucked away in bed."

"All right." What choice did he have but to agree? If he argued too much, then she'd likely sneak off without him, and where would that leave her? Unguarded and likely to be attacked on her way to the tavern, that's where.

She rewarded him with a smile and moved away from her perch to join Phocus at his table. He had arranged a small picnic for them on the ship. Servants brought in freshly roasted fish sprinkled with dill and spices. Eels cooked in milk and honey on platters.

A poet recited an ode to Neptune, and she threw a silver coin at him for his beautiful phrases.

"I could live on a ship," she declared as she bit into a fig.

"You would?" Phocus looked shocked at her side. Not many ladies he knew could live away from their villas.

They did not spend much more time on the ship. Thessalonike made a final tally of ships and things she had seen. Barrels of salted meats and fish were on the dock, ready to be loaded onto ships, but strangely they weren't being hoisted onto merchant ships. Instead, they were being loaded on the galleys. She did not ask Phocus about this. It was better he did not know she even knew the difference and even better if she pretended to be ignorant.

Another day passed, filled with feasts and entertainments, before she had the chance to slip away at night. She had told Aya to give Maro a sign. Aya would remain in her rooms and pretend to be asleep in her bed. If anyone came in all they would see was a sleeping woman, and no one would suspect a thing unless they investigated further.

As dinner drew to a close, Thessalonike made a grand gesture of yawning and looking tired.

She had finally visited the Acropolis and spent the better part of the day visiting the various temples, and she finally saw the Parthenon with its brilliant frieze depicting the procession from the Dipylon Gate to the Acropolis that happened every four years to honor the goddess Athena.

But she had given special attention to the temple of Athena Nike. Located to the right of the main entrance to the Acropolis, it was a simple temple. In the center of the cella that she was allowed to enter was the wingless Nike. She would never be able to fly away, Thessalonike thought, looking at her namesake and feeling a pang in her chest. She wasn't free to leave either.

Duty and responsibility bound her to her family.

Seeing her guest looked so tired, Demetria finally suggested they all retire to their rooms for the evening.

"I apologize for being so exhausted. Perhaps I have been having too much fun. You have been excellent hosts," she complimented the woman.

"Of course, I imagine you shall have much to tell your mother back home. She has been to Athens before, hasn't she? She should visit as well."

"Oh, I doubt she has time between dealing with the Thracians in the north and Alexander in the east."

Demetria's eyes flashed with disapproval. "Surely she cannot be involving herself in the skirmishes and fighting. That's so..." Her voice trailed off. She did not wish to insult her guest, but the word *barbaric* hung between them. Meddling women were not welcome in Athens. She herself was held up as an example to all the wives. Quiet. Meek.

She provided her husband with a son and kept his house in order. She never let a whiff of scandal touch her, nor did her husband have anything to reproach her with. The ideal wife. Many did not even know her name.

"No, of course not. I only meant she has her hands busy with managing the household and palaces. It is hard to keep everything in order." Thessalonike amended the statement, though she wasn't sure the good it did. She kept forgetting how different these Athenian women were. Did they even know how to hold a dagger? How to ride a horse? Were they really as helpless as Demetria seemed to be?

Under the cover of night, dressed in a simple blue dress tied with a leather belt and a brown cloak for warmth, she snuck down the palace corridors. She repeated the instructions in her head. A left at the statue of Aphrodite and another left after she reached the mosaic of the fish swirling around.

Maro was there, dressed in equally unassuming garb. He gave her a quick smile, but they did not speak as he led the way. They left through the servants' gate and disappeared down the street.

"Don't be scared off by foul speech or if you see raucous behavior." He spoke calmly. "Tonight you are not my lady and I am not your guard. Just keep quiet and all should be well. Remember, you wanted this." He repeated himself and sighed as though he was tired already.

"Thank you, Maro." She put a tentative hand on his shoulder. "I know you didn't have to. I promise I won't make a scene."

He nearly flinched at her touch. It was never proper, but he did not shake her off either. "Stay close," he said as they turned onto the street that led to the wine shops and taverns that were already filled with patrons. They stopped in front of a shop with two horses rearing up at each other. Thessalonike studied the crude door, listening to the noises inside.

"They might not be here again."

"It's worth a try." And they went in.

She thanked her lucky stars that she was inconspicuous in her garb among these people who had never seen her before. She was only slightly better dressed than the bar wenches, and besides getting a look here and there hardly anyone paid attention to her. Maro had his arm around her, leading her to a table in the back for some privacy.

"They probably think I'm some common prostitute you hired for the night," she commented as he brought two jugs of wine back from the barkeep.

"I doubt it. They probably think you are my mistress or something like that." His eyes twinkled mischievously. We look more like a pair of young lovers than anything else, hiding from our respective families, he thought to himself.

"So I've been promoted then," she cooed, taking a cup of wine for appearances' sake, although she merely sipped at it. The drink was watered down and not to her taste. In Macedonia, they rarely watered their wines down, but perhaps that was the cause of all the drunken rages that seemed to be commonplace at feasts and banquets.

"Do you see them?" She leaned in and whispered in his ear.

He shook his head. "I didn't think they would be here, but who knows what we will hear? Perhaps we can try another place too."

"You know best." She leaned back, her ears attentive to any information she might overhear.

Maro had downed the first jug of wine and called for another before anything interesting happened.

Four large burly men walked in and began complaining about being run through their paces too much in the last few weeks.

"They're going to tire us out before any fighting will even begin."

"Are you getting old?" His friend clapped him on the back with a heavy hand while the other motioned for a man to bring ale to the table.

"It might not even come to that if the Thracians defeat them."

"Nah, little chance of that. They don't have enough men for the job." Their drinks arrived and the men focused on their drinking.

While that had been the most damning evidence she heard that night, Thessalonike was surprised to hear the common thread between the conversations of disgruntled anger and frustration.

People were upset and angry. These were people ready for a fight.

A few years of peace and prosperity and the Greeks were itching for a fight. She grinned. Alexander would never conquer the world if he could not placate the Greeks.

As they walked back toward the palace, she saw other men and women in the streets. Some men she heard begging for a roll in the hay—just one last time before they got sent off to some war. The women would laugh and say there was no war, but the men grinned and said they would see.

It shocked her to see such open discussions, but she supposed that the commoners rarely had to watch what they said. Who would listen to them?

Well, she was now, and as she made her way back to her rooms she wondered what she would hear in the streets of Pella. There was little chance of her going around unrecognized there, though.

A stone caught in her sandal and she tripped forward, but Maro caught her with one hand and steadied her.

"Drunk already?"

She gave him a light shove. "Don't insult me. I drank more and stronger stuff in Macedonia and did not feel a thing."

He apologized, though she knew he was laughing inwardly at how insulted she felt. Her embarrassment evaporated. She was grateful to Maro. He had been instrumental in helping her gather important information for Olympias.

Whether or not the Athenians would truly betray them and rise up in rebellion was still uncertain, but they were definitely preparing for something.

It amused her to think of how protected her host was trying to keep her. They assumed that distracting her with parties and luxuries would be enough to placate her, but she was more observant than that.

At the end of the week, Thessalonike slipped into a golden dress and gold bangles that went up almost to her elbow. As she looked in the mirror, she thought she looked gaudy, but she did not resist Demetria and Aya as they and a retinue of maids prepared her for the ceremony. She couldn't help but wonder if this splendor would insult the gods, but Demetria assured her that this was necessary.

What girl did not like being decked in jewels? She supposed Thessalonike was not the typical girl. She pursed her lips—if it wasn't for her ancestry and the house she came from, this girl would be an unsuitable wife to her stepson. She would be elevated to one of the first ladies of Athens. A position she was unprepared for.

Dutifully, Thessalonike watched from the sidelines as a representative of her brother carrying his dispatch and permission for the betrothal came forth to shake hands with Phocus. Both men wore ceremonial wreaths, and as their hands clasped the man spoke the words: "I offer her to thee to wife, to get thee lawful children."

Phocus accepted, a small smile on his face as he caught her gaze.

Then the sum of her dowry was rolled out. The amount of gold, jewelry, and land bestowed upon her at the time of their wedding. The land grants were handed over now as a gesture, but everyone knew full well that Phocus would have a hard time claiming them if the wedding did not go through.

It was an unusual arrangement—the dowry was usually paid out now in full, but between the legal complications and the political tension, both sides had agreed to take the cautious route. With the Thracians in open rebellion, the gold could not be transported safely, so it was agreed to be postponed for fear of losing the whole sum. Likewise, the Macedonians were not eager to hand over gold to potential enemies.

The representative had managed to strike up a bargain

that the Athenians would not join Sparta in open rebellion, but words meant nothing.

Thessalonike regarded Phocus without much interest. She supposed she could have found herself a better husband. A king of a distant land, but he was nice enough and easy to manage. She shrugged. Within a few days, she would be boarding a galley heading back to Macedonia posthaste. She might never see him again.

The guests twittered excitedly as the priest finished making the necessary sacrifices for luck and fortune in their marriage—now the party could begin.

Thessalonike sat in the place of honor, Phocus sitting on her right, but they did not share the same couch. Until they were married, it would be improper for them to be seen being too close.

She allowed herself to be fed and entertained, as silent as any statue listening to the men laugh and tease each other. She could be socializing, but she did not feel like it as she looked over the faces of the men who could be plotting to overthrow her brother.

Did they accept money from the Persians to do their dirty work for them? she thought with a sneer.

"Lady Thessalonike, allow me to present Demetrius." Demetria introduced her to a fresh-faced young man. He couldn't be more than twenty-five, but judging from his toga he was already a senator. "He wished to meet the sister of the great Alexander."

"It is an honor." He surprised her by saluting her.

"The honor is mine, I am sure." She sat up straighter, entertained by this man.

Demetrius was certainly an oddity. He had been tasked with giving an epitaph as the food rolled in. She had not paid too much attention, but from what she had heard he had a talent for making speeches.

"I have not heard of your family name before," she said as he took a seat on a stool in front of her.

"I am not surprised, Lady," he said, a gleam of amusement in his eyes. "I came from very humble beginnings, but I had the luck to be educated and taught by Aristotle himself."

"Ah." She was intrigued by him. There was more to his story than just humble beginnings and she noted he had a way with words. He had both bragged about and belittled his accomplishments, adding a little name-dropping as a flourish.

Alexander might have been a pupil of Aristotle at one point, but she knew they did not get along well anymore. She often wondered why there was such a rift between the two men but hardly thought much of it.

"Tell me what your ambitions are for the future." She smiled at Demetrius after the moment of silence that fell between them.

"A forward question, Lady." He winked.

"I am a barbarian princess." She matched his smile with one of her own. "Shall I read your palm? I can see a brilliant future for you. Perhaps you shall climb as high as strategos of Athens one day."

"You flatter me, Lady. I assure you that I have no such goal in mind. I wish only to serve."

"Do you think you'd like to serve my brother? Is that what fascinates you about me?" She was almost bored with him now. Most people seemed to want his favor and a place at his side.

"I am merely curious. He is an oddity in today's world.

Among kings he has become a god and is very well favored by them. I am dabbling in keeping a history and account of the life and times we live in."

"There are plenty of other men who would be much more helpful to you if that is your desire." She took a gulp of the sweet wine and reached for a sweet cake.

"But you are his sister. You must know some tidbit of information about him."

"I rarely saw him. By the time I was old enough to remember, he was studying with Aristotle."

He merely smiled and waited for her to say something else.

"I heard that the actors at the Athenian Theater are some of the best in the whole world. I plan to attend tomorrow night. Do you enjoy the theater?"

"I do."

"Then perhaps we shall speak further there." She grinned and he nodded, bowing to her.

Her eyes followed him as he moved about the hall. He was a keen politician, though what he wanted from her she could only guess. He was an amusing distraction, though. Phocus seemed more engrossed with a young man sitting on his right. Did her betrothed prefer men to women? She sighed, not really caring, but she supposed it was best to be ignored for now. It was her cloak of invisibility.

The parks in Athens were renowned for their beauty. Today with the sun beaming high overhead, the statues sparkled and the fountains shot up a rainbow mist that made the parks seem magical.

Thessalonike walked among them with a retinue of ladies and guardsmen. Phocus had come as well, but he had meandered off in some distant alcove. She did not mind being left to her own thoughts like this.

Tonight she would be dragged along to a theater performance, and then tomorrow she would set sail. Already Aya was overseeing her things being packed away neatly.

She missed home and the security she felt there.

Demetrius surprised her by being there at the entrance to the theater. He would be her escort tonight. Phocus had fallen ill with some sickness, but he had reassured her that he would be well enough to see her off by tomorrow.

Thessalonike replied that she hoped he would get better soon. She knew with a cynical heart that he was likely in bed with someone else or entertaining his friends the way he wished. His father had tried to tame him as a boy, but he still had his appetites and now that he had done his duty he did not see the need to play pretend and act as her lovesick fiancé.

"I did not think you would come," she admitted honestly and she followed after him to the royal box. They would have the best seats in the house.

"I would not miss the opportunity to further speak with you. Perhaps, after you can accompany me to the park?"

She nodded and was surprised to find she could not wait for the play to end.

He was gracious with his compliments, but she couldn't be sure how sincere he was. Perhaps he was trying to seduce her. Thessalonike remembered with a grin how Olympias had warned her of this two years ago.

Never go anywhere alone with a man. Never sleep with a man who was not her husband.

She was to safeguard her virtue as the sister of Alexander. No blemish should be allowed to taint her record.

It wasn't as if Thessalonike did not notice the love bites on Olympias's own neck. She took lovers, why couldn't Thessalonike? But she was not interested in that now. They had left the theater now and were walking with a chaperone.

"You wanted to know more about my brother?" Interrupting whatever Demetrius was going to say.

"Whatever you'd like to tell me." He leaned forward, eager to hear.

"He is like a violent storm, destroying everything in his path. Some may choose to fight against him, but in the end, all shall perish. No one can withstand his fury for long. No one." Now she leaned in—her eyes glazed over. "Not even Sparta."

He coughed in surprise. This he had not been expecting. "You have a gift with words. Perhaps you should become a poetess." He made light of what she had said, but she pressed on.

"Don't fear. All storms end eventually. Then there is peace." She lay back and fanned herself with the peacock fan. "When he was little he used to like to run through vineyards and pick as many grapes as he could. He never dropped one. It caused havoc for the gardeners. You won't find that in any history book."

He grinned. "No, I suppose not."

"Tell me about yourself, Demetrius. How does one go from being nothing to being everything? You must be favored by the gods."

"They gave me a gift," he admitted. "My voice and words seem to carry over crowds and people listen to what

I have to say. I owe my position in life to my voice and the gods that granted it to me."

"A fitting punishment for you then would be to have your tongue cut out." He blanched at her threatening words, but her tone was jovial enough.

"The solution is simple: I shall never do anything to get myself punished."

"That would depend, would it not, on who is judging you."

"You are clever, but I have you there too. I shall simply remain slinking in the shadows."

"Not a noble plan." She stopped midway through her sentence. They had been slowly strolling through the public gardens, and as they turned on the path she caught sight of Maro's familiar form. Pressed up against him and whispering in his ear was some servant girl. Thessalonike quickly turned away from the sight but couldn't stop the feeling of jealousy welling in her throat.

With a smile at her perceived innocence, he moved her along on a different trail. The gardens were a popular place for lovers to meet. "I do not have noble ambitions. Nor do I wish to upset anyone powerful," he finally replied.

"Why did you bother speaking to me?" She couldn't keep the spiteful tone from her voice.

"Well, we shadows need to stick together." He grinned at her expression. "You are powerful in your own way. Many of my compatriots think women are stupid, but I know the truth you are all hiding behind those pretty smiles of yours. Don't worry, I won't tell. I knew from the moment I saw you that you were not some dumb chit. But I do urge you to be careful if you decide to go slumming again."

She hid her gulp of fear well. Olympias would have been proud.

"There you are. See how smart you are. But just remember you are not invisible." He turned and asked his servant walking by for a goblet of wine.

Thessalonike did not beg nor ask him if he was going to expose her. Though there wouldn't be much to expose. All she had done as far as he knew was go for a stroll with her guard. It was shameful but hardly dangerous for her if the news got out.

On top of this, if he was going to expose her, he would have done so already.

"I told you I wanted to know your story, so you had better start talking." She lay back again, unperturbed.

"I suppose fair is fair. Will you promise to remember me when you have returned to Macedonia?"

"Yes." I could hardly forget, she added to herself.

They talked later into the evening. She wasn't even sure she knew what was being said.

That night she went to bed with the dark-haired man imprinted in her mind. He had swept into her life like a hurricane, and in an instant he was gone.

Perhaps he doubted what she could do or he simply did not care, but he had kept his word from the looks of it and had not told anyone anything about seeing her sneaking around at night.

She told Maro about this as the ship pulled them away, and he was antsy the whole trip.

"How could you not have said anything until now?"

"He won't tell."

"You cannot trust him."

"I don't. He's playing his games—I was just a passing

fascination. Why do you look so worried?"

"It would be easy to have you ambushed on board and say that pirates had killed you. Athens wouldn't be blamed and you would be at the bottom of the sea."

Her lips tightened into a thin smile. "I would rather not imagine myself at the bottom of the sea. Thank you very much. If you are so worried, you can go stand guard, but I am telling you I am perfectly safe. Why would he tell me he knows if he was just going to throw me to the dogs anyway?"

Maro did not want to overstep his bounds, and so he saluted her and went off on his own to do just as he said.

Thessalonike couldn't help but feel a bit annoyed with him. It was true he was her guard and was instructed to look after her safety personally, but did he have to treat her like an insufferable child? He was so overbearing at times.

Aya was not sympathetic to her cause. "He cares for you. Don't push him away and teach him that you do not value loyalty or his attention."

"I...you think he cares for me?"

"Of course, you have been his charge for over a year now. You are his mistress, and he has devoted his time to caring for your safety."

"Right. Well, I knew what I was doing in this case. I trust Demetrius—well, I trust him enough that I will not be in any danger of assassination."

Aya was reminded of Tyre but did not say anything.

Annoyed, Thessalonike spent the rest of the trip in the small cabin she had, sulking as she penned a letter to her sisters. They would be curious to hear the news of how her betrothal ceremony went and to hear all about Athens.

5

Pella, 331 BC

"You don't know if it is true. We cannot trust the word of one man." Antipater was arguing against mustering troops to fight against Athens and Sparta.

"You should trust my word then."

Antipater had to hold back a scowl as he regarded Thessalonike, who had stepped forward from the alcove where she was listening.

"I heard and saw men saying the same thing."

"How could you have!?" He seemed surprised.

"I went to see for myself. In disguise, of course," she admitted finally since there was no one here to overhear her confession to Antipater and Olympias.

"You did what?" Olympias was less shocked but still groaned in frustration. "You were supposed to behave."

"I was supposed to gather information," she replied with just as much steel in her voice.

"You were supposed to do nothing but sit beside Phocus and be betrothed," Antipater chimed in.

She shrugged. "I won't say I'm sorry."

Olympias shared a look with Antipater, who rolled his eyes in response.

"Fine. Let us assume you are right. Our forces are spread too thin. We would never be able to hold back the Spartans, Athenians, and the Thracians. Alexander and the main army are too far away, and I can barely muster an army now." Antipater laid out the problem before them.

It wasn't often that he consulted with Olympias, especially not openly, so he was glad that this was a meeting behind closed doors.

"Could the Thracians be reasoned with?" Olympias asked finally after she had paced the length of the room once or twice.

"They could..." Antipater hesitated.

"If we can get them to side with us and put away our quarrels, then we could persevere. The gods are on our side," she added with fervor.

Thessalonike wondered if after years of being called a witch Olympias was starting to believe the lies. If Macedonia fell and lost its foothold in Greece, Alexander's world would collapse around him.

"It might work. I shall speak to the council and begin the talks with the Thracians." Antipater knew that this might very well be their only chance. He couldn't be sure how many troops the Spartans could muster, and then to add Athens into the mix? It was foolish to even consider fighting, but they could not just lay down their swords and give up. He rallied his spirits and tried to regain that youthful spark of bravery and adventure that had always carried him through impossible tasks.

"The information was valuable." He nodded to Thessalonike before bowing to Olympias and leaving the room.

That was all the thanks she would be getting from him, but she didn't mind. She felt helpful.

Maro was at the back of the room and quite forgotten. He had given his report but was not dismissed, so he remained. Thessalonike finally spotted him out of the corner of her eyes and motioned for him to come with her.

Olympias would be at her desk writing out plans and letters. She would be gathering her thoughts and would wish to be by herself for now.

It was late and Thessalonike dragged Maro to an alcove outside. "Thank you for defending me," she whispered and leaned up to place a kiss on his chiseled cheek. He pulled away, shocked by her forwardness.

"What?"

"That is improper."

"You liked it well enough when that slave girl was draped over you."

"That was…I should go." He excused himself and left her alone in the alcove.

She was stunned watching him go. Why had she been so brazen? Her thoughts filled with jealousy at the way he had looked at that girl. His eyes hot with need and desire. He had pushed Thessalonike away, barely meeting her eyes. It stung her pride that he did not seem to like her, as improper and annoying as that would be.

Pella, 327 BC

Olympias was furious and Thessalonike could not seem to calm her. She avoided the items she flung from her desk with expert ease.

"Mother, it will be all right."

"He is ruining everything." Olympias pulled the pin out of her hair and began pulling at her braids in frustration.

Thessalonike released a long sigh.

Word had reached them that Alexander had developed some interesting new habits. Habits he had adopted from the Persians. He no longer seemed content to be seen as a great king; now he wanted to be worshiped as a divine god as well. Supplicants had to bow low to him until their heads touched the ground. No one was allowed to look him in the eye.

People began murmuring that their Greek king was no longer worthy of his title. He was becoming a tyrant.

There was another issue as well.

Alexander had taken a Persian bride. Roxana was rumored to be breathtakingly beautiful, though her father was a mere tribal leader and she hardly seemed a suitable candidate to be chosen as the principal wife of the King of the World.

The Greeks were whispering that they would never let a foreigner rule them. By this they meant any of Roxana's children.

Thessalonike knew there was another reason behind their hatred. For years now they had pressed forward their daughters, and Alexander had not chosen any of them. The trouble was that now the whispers seemed to grow louder. Alexander had been gone from Macedonia for too long.

Olympias had written to him urging him to come home, but he had written back outright refusing.

Thessalonike would never say it out loud, but she knew Olympias was losing her grip on her son.

She had created this self-important, larger-than-life being and he would not be tamed by anyone. Especially not the woman who he now saw as a domineering crone.

"There's a simple solution to all of this." Thessalonike spoke the minute Olympias was quiet.

"What?"

"You need to speak to Antipater. If both of you write to him, then he will have no choice but to listen."

"I will never ask that man for help."

Thessalonike shook her head. "He needs your help just as much as you need his. You have a bargaining chip too. If you put one of his daughters forward as a candidate for Alexander's bride, then he would be indebted to you."

Olympias seemed to calm down as the idea formulated itself in her mind. "You are right, Thessalonike. I have been blinded by fury and did not see. Though I hate admitting I need anything from that man." She scowled.

"That's fine. You don't need to admit anything. But you need to use him. What does it matter which Greek marries Alexander, as long as she comes from a good family? You certainly don't have any candidates, so you might as well reward Antipater. He did squash the Spartan uprising." Thessalonike poured herself a cup of wine. "I can speak to him if you wish. Put the idea in his head too."

Olympias frowned. "Since when did you involve your-self in politics?"

She shrugged. In truth, she was bored and she thought it would be better for her to approach Antipater, knowing she could be more diplomatic. Somehow she had not been tainted by association with Olympias. Though everyone still called Olympias a witch and feared her, they seemed ignorant of Thessalonike, who was just another princess related to Alexander.

She had escaped the confines of the castle and was basking in the hot sun. Something she wasn't supposed to do, but she didn't care too much about what was considered proper. Nor did she care if she burned in the sun.

Thessalonike was reminded of Cynane, who had always tossed the rules aside, but everyone thought she was beautiful. There was something wild about her half-sister.

Now her sister was a mother herself. No doubt teaching her daughter the ways of the warrior, just as she had been raised.

Maro tossed her a plum and she caught it.

"Are you sure you don't want me to teach you how to swim?" he asked. This had been the official excuse for her leaving the palace. Aya had come too, but she was over with the horses.

"No. I am sure Lady Olympias knows I just needed a reason to escape. You could have taught me in a pool—we didn't have to come to the sea."

"True." He kicked at the sand with his foot.

She did have another motive for dragging him out here where there was no one to hear them over the crashing waves and the strong but cool wind. They had not talked since her outburst and he was polite enough not to bring it up, but she wanted to now.

She had no right to keep him away from anyone. She

had no claim to him nor could she. Her childish crush had to be put aside.

"I would like to talk to you," she began but then bit into the plum, juices coating her hand. "I am sorry I yelled at you and sorry I kissed your cheek. I probably drank too much."

He coughed nervously, casting a look around the beach to see if anyone was nearby.

"Maro, please forgive me. Am I really so ugly you pushed me away?" she begged again. She did not want to cry. Did he hate her so much and find her so repulsive? Was he only being polite because of who she was?

Maro regarded her with surprise from his vantage point. He could see how her lower lip quivered, a sure sign she was holding back tears.

"Please..." The word came out a whisper that the wind carried away.

In that moment, he was no longer Maro the soldier with dreams of fighting in a far-off battle. He was a man before a beautiful woman he admired.

He knelt before her, taking her hands in his. "There is nothing to forgive," he assured her. "You are breathtaking. Surely you must know that."

She laughed and pulled her arms away. A few tears escaped her eyes and she wiped them away.

"You are teasing me."

"You are the one who has always teased me. I am yours to command," he said hotly.

"There are plenty of girls throwing themselves at you. Or do you want me to..." He silenced her with a kiss on the lips. It was brief and lasted all of a second, but it sent tingles down her spine, numbing her to all else.

"I have committed what some might call treason. So now my life is truly in your hands." He was still on his knees in the sand, and she got off the chair she was sitting on to kneel before him too.

"I fear I have grown to see you as more than just my friend and protector." She looked him in the eye as she spoke, and she was surprised to see the joy in his eyes at her confession. "What am I going to do?"

He grinned and kissed her again. This time longer and they did not separate until they heard footsteps coming down the path, kicking up stones.

Thessalonike was back in the chair in an instant and Maro was on his feet, but still Aya was not fooled. She looked at the pair of them and saw their flushed cheeks and her mistress's bruised lips.

"How are the lessons going?"

"Quite well." Thessalonike threw on her veil again.

"I thought you needed to get in the water to learn how to swim." Aya was quite cheeky.

"Oh sit down, Aya. Why don't you tell me more about how your Egyptians think the world was made?"

The whole time Aya talked, Thessalonike kept sneaking glances at Maro and they smiled at one another. But it did give her time to think. What could their relationship be? Maro was the fourth son of a poor nobleman in Thrace who had lost his lands. He barely had any aristocratic blood to scrape together, and what about power or wealth? He had none. There was nothing to entice Olympias to allow the match.

Thessalonike gulped at that thought. Would she run away? Duty prevented her from doing such a thing.

Besides, where would they go? To Rome? What kind of life would they have? That dream ended just as quickly.

No, they would have to make do with secret meetings and stolen glances. The methodical person inside her head said that was for the best, but Thessalonike's heart couldn't help but seize in her throat.

"I think Aya is right." Maro's voice broke her reverie.

"What?" She blinked, confused by his question.

"You should be initiated into the sea. Perhaps the more you are familiar with it the less you will be frightened by it."

"No! I cannot." She leaped to her feet, but she was not fast enough and he grasped her by her waist and threw her over his shoulders, already plodding closer to the sea.

She squirmed, trying to get away. Half out of hysterical laughter and half out of fear.

"Do you trust me?" he asked as he shifted her so she slid off into his arms. He was now holding her bridal style.

She looked into his dark eyes, mesmerized by them, and finally nodded. Only then did he drop them in. She hadn't even noticed he had carried them deep enough so the water came up to his shins.

The water was cold and the waves threatened to pull her out of his arms and send her tumbling.

She was afraid, but as the grip around her tightened the fear went away.

Suddenly, they were out of the water again. She was soaked through. Her gray chiton clung to her.

Maro let her down at the edge of the water, the waves barely touching her feet. Now that she was in the sun she wasn't so cold anymore, though she missed being held in his arms.

"How was that, milady?" Aya came laughing but also concerned. Perhaps their joking had gone too far.

"I don't know if I'll ever learn how to swim properly, but it was refreshing." She struggled to find an appropriate word.

Aya helped adjust her gown. Typically people swam naked for sport in bathhouses and gymnasiums, but it was hardly suitable here.

They waited until her gown had dried enough to not look unseemly and they headed back to the citadel.

That night after the other maids had been dismissed, Aya approached her mistress with a small pouch.

"I don't know what is going on between you while you were alone, but if you do not want an accident you must drink a tea made out of these leaves every day."

"Whatever for?" Thessalonike did not quite catch on.

"To prevent an accident."

Suddenly it dawned on her and she blushed beet red. "You cannot think..."

Aya shrugged. "I am just urging you to be cautious. I am sorry if I have offended you." She pulled away the outstretched pouch, but Thessalonike stopped her.

"I'll take it. Just in case. You went through all the trouble of getting it, after all." She tried to come up with a thousand excuses, but now it was Aya's turn to silence her.

"I cannot tell you what to do, nor will I judge you, but remember that the path you are taking is a difficult one and you must be prepared to put it aside. I won't be the one to betray you, but there are eyes and ears all over the palace." She gave a last warning to her mistress before bowing and bidding her good night.

Thessalonike lay awake for quite some time thinking

about what she had said. It would be scandalous if she was discovered—Maro would be sent away—was it worth it? Memories of the kiss they had shared earlier and the way she felt in his arms reassured her. He could leave or stop this whenever he wanted, but she would not be the one to do it. She was old enough now to know the ways of the world.

She was nearly twenty-one, and so far none of her betrothals had amounted to anything. She wanted love. She was ready for it. She wasn't betraying anyone.

With that settled, she lay down and slept.

❦

Epirus, 327 BC

Fortuna had smiled upon her and her newfound love.

Her sister had sent a missive to her mother asking her for assistance in Epirus, but Olympias was too busy to go at the moment and so had decided to send Thessalonike to see what she could do.

It had been nearly ten years since Thessalonike had seen her sister. Now she was ruling as regent for her infant son after her husband's untimely death.

Thessalonike's mind was not on how she could help her sister but rather on the fact that she would have more opportunities to be alone with Maro. They would be away from Pella and the watchful eyes ready to report to Olympias.

Aya, who was still as disapproving as ever, would be there to help her have secret rendezvous with her lover.

The journey west took several days, but they dared not meet in private.

It was only upon arriving at the capital city Passaron and greeting her sister that she was able to sneak off with him to meet in the public park like any other shameless woman with a lover.

"Shouldn't you be helping your sister write missives to the Molossian council?"

"She can spare me for a few hours." She sighed as she nuzzled his neck. Then she looked up at him and smiled. "Or are you done with me now?"

"Never." He grinned and soon they lost another hour in each other's arms.

Aya was waiting for her, looking anxious in her rooms.

"Your sister came looking for you," she said, noting Thessalonike's disheveled appearance with a frown. "You should go to her rooms after I'm done rearranging your gown."

"Thank you, Aya."

"You should not leave for so long next time or she might send soldiers to find you."

"I am sorry."

"Don't apologize to me. I am just warning you."

Thessalonike found her sister pacing her private rooms. In the dim light of the lamps, she looked like the spitting image of Olympias when she was younger.

"You wanted to see me?"

Cleopatra rounded on her. "Where have you been?"

"Exploring. What happened?"

Cleopatra did not believe her for a second, but there were more pressing matters to deal with at the moment.

"The Chaonian leader has gone to the Thesprotians behind my back."

Thessalonike's eyebrow rose, indicating she should continue.

"They are setting up a league against me."

"Are you sure you aren't jumping to conclusions?"

"Nikanor has never liked me." Cleopatra all but pouted in frustration. "What am I going to do? You are no help to me and I shall lose my throne."

"Your son's throne," Thessalonike corrected unsympathetically. "It is not my fault you have made a mess of ruling your kingdom and angered your allies."

Her sister glowered at her and asked through gritted teeth what she should do then.

"If they are planning to create a league, then make sure you are involved and are in control. You must find a way to make them your friends again. For now, you still hold the upper hand. Don't let them take it away from you. Be nice."

Cleopatra bit her lower lip, considering this. Tonight she had let her frustration turn her into an errant child. She was always impatient to get what she wanted. "Fine. I will think about it."

"Do you want me to sit with you and go over documents?" Thessalonike asked and when her sister nodded took a seat at the desk and waited.

She stayed for three weeks with Cleopatra, trying to help her navigate the tumultuous political situation in Epirus. Her sister had always been too power hungry and aggravated the other powerful tribes in the region, but soon she was on her way back home.

The camp was quiet as a man moved stealthily among

tents. It was late and almost everyone was asleep except for the guards stationed on lookout around the perimeter.

He was supposed to be getting some sleep himself, but he had something to do first.

He pushed back the tent flap and was nearly thrown back out when a body launched itself at him. Thessalonike was not small. Her lithe form was hardened by exercise and she was tall for a woman.

"Maro, I thought you wouldn't come tonight," she whispered as she nuzzled his neck.

"I couldn't let this chance pass. It would have been harder if we made it to some noble's home and rested there for the night."

"Hush, now." She stopped his excuses with a kiss and pulled him to her makeshift bed. Aya had already slipped out and would stand watch outside. What would she do without her loyal servant? Thessalonike made a mental note to reward her with a gift once they got back to Pella.

In an instant, her gown was off and they writhed in bed, finding pleasure in each other.

They lay for a moment side by side after the heat of their lovemaking had dissipated. His hands tracing circles down her back.

"We should have stayed longer in Epirus," she groaned.

"No matter." He placed a kiss on her forehead, feeling the exhaustion creep up on him. "I have to tell you something."

"What?"

"I have decided to speak to my superior to send me out to the main army when they send the next batch of reserve troops."

She sat up. "Whatever for?"

"Glory. Honor. Take your pick. I must find a way to make a name for myself in this world."

She pulled up her gown, covering her naked form once more. "Have you tired of me already? I can speak to my mother if you wish. I am sure I can arrange a post for you."

He shook his head, almost insulted she would suggest such a thing.

Finally, she nodded, knowing there was not much she could say to keep him by her side. This was their best chance. She would have to let him go.

Pella, 325 BC

They were shocked by the news. Olympias had almost fainted, but she managed to compose herself before the messenger and sent him off to the kitchens to get a good meal.

"Thessalonike." She tightened her grip on her arm to the point of bruising it. "Tell me he will live."

"He will. He has the best doctors looking after him. If he was so weak and close to death he would not have been able to write to you himself," she assured her mother.

The god king no longer seemed divine. He himself had declared to his soldiers, "See this blood. I am but a man."

They were worried for him though, and the world seemed to wait with bated breath to see what would happen next. It was hard to tell. Perhaps the wound would fester and the infection would kill him.

But a few weeks later it was clear that he was on the mend. The physicians had done their work well.

Thessalonike sat at her writing desk wondering if her brother was truly unstoppable. His luck never seemed to run out. Perhaps Olympias was right and he would conquer the world before he stopped.

This had been a bad year for Alexander. His wife Roxana had lost their first child. His famous horse Bucephalus had died the year before as well. These were not the best omens, but Alexander did not seem to be slowing down.

She was busy with her thoughts and allowed Aya to run off with her husband. The man was a servant too, working in the blacksmith shop, but Aya seemed content with her lot. Thessalonike had promised she would never separate them. Though for now she couldn't promise their freedom. Aya had not dared to bring it up, though she claimed to be more than happy where they were now.

In the six years she had served her, Aya had proven her loyalty over and over again. Thessalonike swore she would be rewarded for her years of service. She was more of a friend now than anything else.

For now, she put aside her writing and had the sudden urge to work at the loom. The new red cloth she was making was getting longer and longer. Soon it would be the proper length for a gown. She was proud of her own work, for she had poured her heart into every stitch. Maro was in her thoughts every time she sat in front of the loom and touched the threads.

Occasionally, she would receive word from him. He wrote to Aya under the guise of being her lover, and she passed on the letters to Thessalonike.

She ached for him and longed to see him again.

It had been nearly two years since he had left.

Pella, 324 BC

When she awoke that morning, she did so with a sense of dread.

She did not push away the blankets even as the servants trailed in. They avoided meeting her gaze and she ignored them.

She had committed a crime yesterday and the whole world knew it. She had dared to question the great king—not only her brother but also a god.

There was no pity for her.

She felt as though the word *traitor* had been stamped on her forehead.

The truth was that she had been furious and crazed with heartbreak, though there was no way she could have admitted that to her cohorts, much less her adopted mother. How could she tell them she had loved a man who was first her guard then a soldier in her brother's army? How could they understand the pain that overwhelmed her after she had finished reading his latest letter? He was going to be promoted to captain—he would earn the right to marry her. Now he had been buried in some distant field. Killed by an arrow. It went through his neck as he fought with another man. His helmet had fallen off. That was not the way he was supposed to die.

Thessalonike felt the tears well in her eyes again. She thought they had been spent, but it seemed they had rejuvenated themselves. She hid her face in the silk pillows and let them out in choking sobs.

Alexander would be preparing for the wedding

feasts at Susa. He had picked two brides for himself, and his commanders had been paired off with Persian brides as well. It was an effort to show that the two cultures were now united. The Greeks and the Persians.

Alexander was trying to mix oil and water.

He had performed miracles in the past, so why not this too?

But Thessalonike knew things that Olympias and Alexander did not know or were blind to.

The Greeks were too proud. These marriages would be seen as an insult to their heritage. Their forefathers had vanquished Xerxes from Greece. Now they were expected to marry their enemies? No. They would not stand for this.

Rebellions had sprung up for much less.

But Alexander had his friends around him, and with their support and love surrounding him he had become blind to such things.

He had squashed rebellion after rebellion. "Let them come," he would hiss as he tried to impose his idea of a perfect world on an imperfect people.

The Persians she was certain would be insulted that they were being forced to mix their blood with what they saw as lesser beings. Greeks were savages to them.

Thessalonike loved her brother, but she hated the king —the son of a god who wouldn't listen to reason.

She had tried to warn her brother, but the king had gotten in the way.

Perhaps Olympias would have her killed for the words she had shouted at her yesterday.

She didn't know how long she remained in bed for, but

when Aya stormed in followed by a handful of servants, Thessalonike propped herself up on her elbows.

"It's time for you to get up, Princess," she scolded, pulling the covers off Thessalonike.

She directed the other servants to come forth with a platter of food while the rest went around the room opening the windows and tidying up. Thessalonike blinked. When had she thrown her food to the ground? She noticed the platter from this morning lying across the room.

Aya fed her herself, watching every bite of food she took and making sure Thessalonike swallowed it.

Once she was done, Aya dragged her off to the bath-house. There Thessalonike was scrubbed from head to toe and put in a clean himation gown as her hair was combed and braided.

"I can't imagine Antipater is too happy with me right now." She broke the silence. Aya shrugged. "From what I have heard, he does not disagree with you."

The words shocked Thessalonike, but they shouldn't have. Antipater liked to argue with Olympias.

"Was she very furious? Did you see her face?"

"She was silent, but that was probably because she was shocked after your outburst. I imagine you are lucky you did that in her rooms and not in the throne room in front of all the courtiers."

"The slaves heard—it's probably all over the palace now." Thessalonike sighed and wondered what she would do. Should she apologize?

"They've been silenced, but people do know you fell ill and went into a craze of emotions."

"Over what?"

Aya grinned. "Your love Hephaestion is marrying another woman and has forsaken you. The news shocked you."

Thessalonike laughed until the tears came to her eyes. The embarrassment was her punishment, it seemed. It was neater this way. In one smooth motion, Olympias had ensured her words would be disregarded. Nothing more than the ravings of a grief-stricken woman. The irony was not lost on her either, for it was true she was grief-stricken but she wasn't blind either. She wondered if this was how Cassandra felt in her tower in Troy—able to see the future but with no one to believe her.

Now she cried for Maro again. She could see him in her mind, the hapless way he would smile at her. His caresses and touches. Now he was gone—curse Alexander. She couldn't stop herself as the evil treacherous thoughts crossed her mind.

Perhaps Olympias would be right to have her executed. She was a traitor, even if it was just in her mind.

"You are to recover a few days at Aigai. I will accompany you. Then you can return." Aya put a hand on her friend's shoulder. She didn't know the whole story, but she had walked in on her crying over a letter, repeating the words *he's dead* over and over again.

Perhaps a lover or a secret betrothal? She wasn't sure, but she didn't ask either. That wasn't her way.

"I need to speak to her before I leave. Will she see me?" Thessalonike wiped away the fresh tears with the back of her hand. She hadn't cried this much since she was a little girl. Now at twenty-four, she could no longer hide behind the excuse of her age.

"I am sure she will." Aya bit her lip. "You won't yell again, will you?"

Thessalonike shook her head. "I promise I will not."

She allowed her friend and companion to lead her to Olympias's rooms. They waited on stools for nearly an hour before they were given admittance. Thessalonike had not dared to stroll into her mother's rooms like she usually did. After the outburst yesterday, she was surprised she had not awoken in a dungeon.

A slave held the door open and Thessalonike walked in, head held high despite her red eyes and tear-streaked face.

Olympias regarded her silently for a moment, and seeing the coldness in her eyes, Thessalonike fell to her knees, shocking the woman. "I was wrong."

She did not apologize—that would be a greater lie and empty words to this woman.

"Stand up," Olympias commanded, but Thessalonike remained where she was until she felt the familiar hands grasp her by the shoulders and allowed herself to be hauled up. "We shall never speak of this again, and you will never betray me like that again," Olympias whispered into her hair as she hugged her tightly.

"No." She cried in the arms of the woman who called her daughter. She did not argue that she had not betrayed her—it seemed that Olympias now thought that contradicting her was a betrayal.

"We are bound together by blood and destiny. I love you, but never hurt me like that again," Olympias went on to say. "Now you shall go to Aigai and recover from whatever it is that seems to ail you. You cried those tears for someone else, not me." She was still as perceptive as ever. "Return when you have composed yourself."

Thessalonike gave a little bow, something she was not used to doing to the woman who she called mother, but she was observing all decorum now.

With that, she returned to her rooms in a great hurry. Aya barely had time to pack a chest of her things before she pulled her into the litter with her and Phila, Antipater's eldest daughter, who had volunteered to come with her.

She didn't need her fancy gowns and jewelry where she was going.

The trio traveled in relative silence. Only Phila spoke once in a while with their retinue's captain to see how long they had to go.

Thessalonike was just trying to hold back the tears and the rage. Her life wasn't supposed to be like this. She had gone to the astrologer and he had said she would be married soon and that she would have three sons. Usually, they said only two, so she thought he might have had a true vision. She pictured Maro with their little children around him.

She had held on to that future like a naïve fool.

Astrologers always read marriage and children in the palms of rich unmarried women. Liar. She thought of the man with such hate, but in truth she was mad at herself for letting this all happen.

At least if he could have been allowed to live, then...her thoughts trailed off as the carriage came to a stop. Were they here already?

She was the first to climb out of the carriage. The palace steward had come down the steps bowing and bidding her welcome. Slaves carrying bowls filled with rose water to wash her hands and feet approached. She let them pamper her, then allowed Phila and Aya to pull her along to her rooms.

Only Aya knew the true reason behind her visit here but was sure she would recover given a moment of reprieve. Phila, noticing the princess's dour mood, did not mention that her father had told her Alexander was thinking of marrying her off to some Persian king. Aya had scowled when she whispered this news to her. Well, her mistress had been betrothed other times too and the wedding had never happened. Perhaps she was cursed.

When this whole debacle had begun with Maro, Aya had warned her that this would never work and that she had better safeguard her heart, but Thessalonike had been young and eager. Nothing could touch her. It was as though she was the first woman to ever feel love.

Aya had allowed her to bask in the happiness of her love. Then Maro had enlisted in the army, trying to find a way to earn prestige and honor. What had that gotten him? Sent to the army in Syria—dead within three years of his departure.

Thessalonike could not nurse her broken heart forever, not now when rebellion hung in the air. When courtiers were plotting and the royal family was divided. It seemed clear that Alexander had no intention of ever returning to Macedonia.

Even Aya knew that would spell disaster.

Slowly Thessalonike began to emerge from the hole she had dug herself into. She locked away Maro in the back of her mind. There was no sense mourning the dead forever when there was so much for the living to do—or at least that's what she repeated to herself over and over again.

Every day he seemed a bit further away and she began asking for missives from the court.

She would stay abreast of everything that was happening as she tried to forget the way Maro's hands would caress hers or the way he had held her in a tight embrace before he left with one last final kiss on her lips.

She had been angry with him and she had pushed him away. She thought of this as she reached for yet another scroll to look over. She was good with the accounting and keeping track of the grain supply coming in from Egypt. There were slaves and stewards whose sole job was to look over this, but she felt it gave her purpose, and besides she had a vested interest in making sure the numbers were correct.

When she wasn't locked up in her rooms with her scrolls, she worked at the loom with Phila. They managed to get three inches of fine cloth done. It was only later that she noticed she had picked a deep red silk.

"Another wedding veil?" Aya asked in a teasing way. She looked guilty almost instantly, but Thessalonike laughed. "I had not noticed, but I suppose it could be." She ran her fingertips over the smooth silk.

Aya and Phila shared a glance with each other. She is mending, their gazes seemed to say with some relief.

Some women were eaten away by grief until it consumed them, but Thessalonike was made of sterner stuff.

❧ 6 ❧

Pella, 324 BC

She was petting Zephyrus, his velvet nose pressed against her cool hand in a familiar fashion.

She enjoyed spending time with him, though she rarely had time to go running down trails with him like she used to.

She was tired lately and she didn't know why. Perhaps she was catching some sickness.

Turning around at the sound of approaching footsteps, Thessalonike was surprised to find Aya standing there with her short hair wet from the bathhouse.

"Is something wrong?" Usually, Aya did not wander around the halls without her wig.

"Lady Olympias was looking for you."

"Ah. I shall be right there." She looked at her again. "Is something wrong?" she asked again.

"No, it is just the servant that sent me to look for you

seemed impatient to find you. I suppose it is something urgent."

Thessalonike patted Zephyrus's head again and left the stables, heading down the corridors to the familiar rooms.

She ran across Antipater and Craterus with their heads together as though they were whispering secrets to one another. What were they plotting? Ever since Craterus had returned with the veterans, he had attached himself to Antipater's side.

Antipater nodded to her and Craterus followed suit. The old general had a kindly face, unlike Antipater, who looked more and more sullen these days. She knew that Olympias was behind it. As she always was—she seemed to have made it her goal to bring down Antipater.

Craterus had always bickered with Hephaestion—they argued over Alexander's policy of integrating the Persians and Greeks. But he did not seem happy about the news.

What Thessalonike did not tell Olympias was that even if Antipater was removed, another man would take his place as regent. The Macedonians would never allow Olympias to be the regent. She had often wished the two of them could get along, but that did not seem to be the case.

She barely avoided the servants rushing from her mother's rooms and she peeked inside to find her leaning against the wall, her hand massaging her temple.

"Mother?"

"Come in, Thessa." She used her old childish nickname. "It seems Hephaestion has perished from a fever."

"Hephaestion?" Thessalonike was shocked. Alexander must be devastated.

"Yes, Alexander is preoccupied with his grief now. He

consulted with an oracle to grant Hephaestion divine status. He is making some plans to build a temple too. He is losing his loyal followers. One by one."

Thessalonike did not think so. There were plenty of his old friends still loyal to him. But she saw what Olympias was concerned about. There had been setbacks as well as victories this year, but it seemed as though recently nothing was going the way it should. Alexander should have had an heir. He also should have agreed to marry Antipater's daughter.

Thessalonike thought of the kind and gentle Phila and believed that they would not have made a good match. Alexander, from what she knew of him and what she had heard, had become a tough man—his mind was on victory and conquest.

It was Phila who approached her with a request a few days later.

"My sister, Nicaea, is struggling at home. I wonder if you might agree to take her on as your companion."

"That is a peculiar request." Thessalonike frowned, though she wouldn't mind having another companion now that Phila would soon be married again.

"My mother is not feeling well," Phila admitted. "She's a nice girl, but she is twelve years old and is likely to misbehave."

"You are being too honest, Phila. How do you expect me to agree now?" Thessalonike laughed but agreed to her request.

Nicaea arrived at the palace gaping like the child she was. She took to Thessalonike with surprising ease, becoming her shadow and trying to emulate her in every way.

"I don't know why she does that." Thessalonike found it flattering as well as peculiar.

"You are a royal princess. Of course she wishes to emulate you. She's not the only one either. You just haven't noticed," Aya pointed out.

They enjoyed a few months of peace before the world seemed to come crashing down.

❦

Pella, 323 BC

The news, which she knew was coming or at least would at some point, had finally reached Pella.

The city was silent. Disbelief was in the air. Alexander the Great was dead. He had not died in battle; he died of fever.

His light had burned out faster than it should have, but he had also accomplished more in his life than others did in generations.

Olympias was inconsolable, and Thessalonike stayed in her room with her lyre, striking the same tragic tune over and over again as she sat deep in thought.

Roxana was four months pregnant. She could be carrying the only legitimate son of Alexander, and he would be heir to the throne if he survived. But she was not in Macedonia, and it was likely she would never live to see it.

Thessalonike strummed again.

She could only imagine Alexander's generals and commanders fighting over his body, each trying to claim a piece of the mighty empire he had built. It stretched from the Indian Ocean to Greece. There was enough to go around, but she was certain that there would still be fighting.

Men always seemed to fight.

She strummed her lyre again. More harshly this time.

Antipater was somewhere in the palace now. Dredging up support, no doubt. He had been supposed to lead the legions to fight in Asia, but now that Alexander was dead he was sure to try to retain his title as regent of Macedonia.

She strummed her lyre again.

Perhaps that would no longer be good enough for him. Why be a regent when you could be a king? But Antipater was an honorable man—she doubted he would take that step. Still, she shivered as she thought of what the future would bring. It seemed bleak to her now, and she knew that if power was not consolidated quickly, she would be in trouble. Everyone who had Alexander's blood in their veins would be.

She strummed her lyre again. Fortuna's wheel was churning rapidly. It was getting ahead of her, and she could not see what to do.

She could find safety with Cleopatra or Cynane. She drew in her breath. Would Cynane make a play for the throne? Her daughter was now fifteen, and perhaps she would marry her off to the next king with her soldiers at her back. She could muster and lead troops to fight with her.

Cleopatra was in her rooms plotting. Sometimes she looked like a dark-haired version of Olympias. Plotting over her scrolls and with her ladies. She was sharp and quick-witted, always on the lookout for some way to profit and increase her power. But unlike her mother, she seemed unable to successfully hold any power she gained.

Olympias had to go to Epirus to rule on her behalf after a falling out with the other noble families. Cleopatra could have ruled until her son reached his majority, but she had overstepped her boundaries and lost all her power.

She strummed her lyre again.

For the first time in years, she thought of her father and the bloodbath that had ensued. She had been young and traumatized, but now she understood why it had happened. Why it had been necessary. But it still scared her that now they would be required to fight and kill once more.

She strummed her lyre yet again.

Aya walked in with a tray of warmed soup and a jug of wine.

"You need to eat."

Thessalonike blinked in confusion.

"You have not eaten since yesterday," Aya pressed. "You will need your strength."

Thessalonike looked at the soup and bile rose in her throat. She was not hungry, nor was she ready to eat just yet. There was so much to think about. So much to plan. The worry in Aya's eyes stopped her. Finally, she made herself reach down and take the bowl in her hands. She ate it quickly, her hunger returning with each spoonful, and then she drank the wine. It stilled her mind and helped calm her. She had not realized how much she was shaking. Had she gone mad?

"Do you know what will happen?" Aya's question was soft, but the anxiety in her voice was clear.

Thessalonike shook her head. "No."

"Praxus wants us to leave if it is possible. We can go to a little cottage in the foothills and wait until it is all over."

Thessalonike feared this would be the case. She had promised Aya that she could leave whenever she wanted to, but now that she was asking she was terrified to let her leave. Aya had been a constant friend and companion and now she would be alone.

"Stay a bit longer. Until we know what is happening, but you can go the minute there is trouble," she finally said, and Aya looked relieved.

"I would not abandon you, but..." She placed a hand over her lower stomach.

"You are with child?" Thessalonike was surprised.

Aya gave a little smile. "It's still early, but Praxus is worried for me."

Thessalonike nodded. "You shall be safe. I will make sure you have enough money to live comfortably." She bit her lip. Would she have anything to give her in a few days?

She walked over to her jewelry box and picked up several gold bangles. "Sell them and keep the money. I may have more to give you later."

"That is too generous." Aya gaped at them. She had been given a small fortune.

"Take it." Thessalonike now wished to know what Antipater was doing. "I am going to go see my mother," she lied, and the two women separated.

Everyone in the palace was dressed in black. As Thessalonike approached the throne room, she imagined she looked like a pale ghost with her black hair. Antipater was there, trying to ease the concerns of the people. Thessalonike watched him through the doorway. He must be worried because he had sent his daughters away. She missed Nicaea most of all, having grown attached to the girl.

Finally, she slid into the room, following behind a few slaves carrying in scrolls and food. He was bent over a great table usually used during banquets, looking at letters with another man she did not recognize.

She watched them for a moment before he noticed her.

"Princess, you should not be here. I have heard you were unwell."

"I am better now." She held back the question she meant to ask, not daring to voice her concerns.

"We are taking care of things. The Athenians are threatening to rise up and we are planning a defense. Nothing to concern yourself over." Antipater knew she was concerned despite his words, but she nodded and left the hall, knowing when she wasn't wanted.

This was a man's world, and there was little she could do officially. Olympias would be here soon—she would know what to do, if grief over the loss of her son had not claimed her.

Thessalonike would have to wait. They all would have to wait.

In the months that followed, it seemed as though nothing else could shock her. Ptolemy had whisked away Alexander's sarcophagus, which was making its way back to Macedonia. Olympias had sent him a few pleading letters, but he had not budged and she dropped the matter.

Of course, Thessalonike was sure she was plotting something, but then again maybe she just wanted her son to be at peace.

The marriage proposals flooded in for Cleopatra's hand. As the only fully related sister of Alexander the Great, she would provide an advantageous marriage on several fronts.

Her son sat on the throne in Epirus.

She had a fortune for a dowry, and even more than that she would give tremendous amounts of prestige to any man who married her.

She walked around the palace sighing heavily about the serious choices she had to make. All the while, Cleopatra carried the letters from her potential suitors around with her as though they were her trophies. She made promises to all of them but had not settled on anyone yet. This game was too tempting for her to resist. She had become a young girl again and found herself highly desirable.

For once Thessalonike was not jealous of her elder sister. She would prefer to be forgotten. Anyone who would marry her would only be vying for a claim on the throne. Fortuna had not favored her with a marriage, but this allowed her the peace of working at the loom, playing her lyre, or working on medicines.

Her heart had been given away a long time ago, and now she had no lofty ambitions or desire to marry.

News reached them that Cynane had crossed the sea into Asia. She brought Eurydice, her daughter, with her along with a small army. Their intent was clear—they were heading to meet Phillip Arrhidaeus, their half-brother, who was recently declared king of Macedonia.

Thessalonike bit her lip nervously. This could not end well for her. Cynane had never seemed ambitious, but now it seemed to have infected her. Olympias rounded on her servants when the news was brought to her. Traitor. The word hissed out.

In the end, Olympias did not have to do anything. Perdiccas took matters into his own hands. He sent his brother Alcetas with an army to stop her.

In a brave effort to give her daughter a fighting chance to meet up with Phillip, Cynane stood and fought him head-on. She died a warrior's death, brave and composed.

Thessalonike remembered how Cynane had fought off the Illyrians at the head of her own army. The men had celebrated her for days as a great general. They applauded the way she had savagely killed the Illyrian Queen Caeria and attributed their victory to her.

She had always been ruthless. Always charging into battle alongside her men. Perhaps if she had been born a man, she would have been an even greater force to contend with than Alexander.

Thessalonike was not sure where she drew such strength and bravery from. But it did not matter now. Cynane was dead.

Her daughter had managed to escape, and the marriage ceremony was conducted without delay. Thessalonike thought of the niece she had never seen with worry—she had been pushed forward in this game, and if she did not win she would perish alongside her mother.

Antipater had reason to be concerned now, but at least he did not have to worry about Olympias for once. She seemed to be staying out of the fighting for now. Her attention was firmly on Roxana and her young son.

Sometimes Thessalonike would come across her cradling the child to her breast, whispering to him the great exploits of his father.

"You shall finish what he started," she whispered to the babe and kissed his forehead. She spotted Thessalonike and motioned her forward.

"Doesn't he look just like him?" She had not said her son's name since his passing. Only Thessalonike noticed the way she avoided it and the way the corners of her lips twitched at the mention of him. She was grieving but was hiding it quite well.

Life had to go on.

"He does. Have you seen his future?" she asked just as quietly so she wouldn't disturb the sleeping child.

"I don't need to. He will grow into a soldier. I can tell." Olympias had an almost crazed look in her eyes as she smiled up at Thessalonike. "I will see he comes to his throne." She did not say no matter what, but by now Thessalonike knew how she operated in absolutes. Nothing would stand in her way.

Roxana appeared from her room, rubbing her groggy eyes. "Alexander?" Her accent was thick as she asked for her son.

Olympias handed the baby to her and left to go plod around her rooms. She had not said anything about Cynane's death, but it seemed to everyone that she was looking relieved as of late.

Thessalonike suspected she had been the one to warn Perdiccas of Cynane's plot. Olympias's hand was usually found meddling in everyone's affairs. Sometimes Thessalonike wondered how she had managed to consolidate so much power, but she knew it was better not to know. She feared to implicate herself in affairs as serious as these. More importantly, she did not wish to participate in making war on her brothers and sisters. They were family, but you wouldn't know it from looking at them.

She left the suspicious but beautiful Roxana with her baby and returned to her own safe rooms.

Nicaea was waiting for her. She knew her well enough by now to know she came to talk.

So taking a seat across from her, Thessalonike asked her what was on her mind.

Nicaea seemed to have trouble meeting her eyes. "I am being sent away to Asia. My father wants me to marry Perdiccas."

Thessalonike's eyes widened in shock, but quickly she hid her surprise. While she was young, it was not terribly unusual to be married so soon. It would be a good match. She shouldn't be surprised and made her opinion known. "You would be wife to the regent of Macedonia, an honor."

"Father just wants to consolidate his hold over Perdiccas. You know they've always fought with each other. My father has never forgiven him for replacing him as regent."

"That was only because of my mother's scheming. Alexander respected him greatly," Thessalonike interjected.

Nicaea shook her head. "He told me that Perdiccas wants to claim the empire as his own. He wants to use me as a bargaining chip to stop his plots. He wants me to persuade him."

Thessalonike blinked. This was news to her, but then again she had not preoccupied herself too much with listening to the gossip or news around the court.

"I cannot do it." Nicaea's tears spilled down her face in a steady stream, but as always she cried silently. It was true, her little companion had never been one to be influential, nor was she outspoken. Most would call her the ideal woman—silent and obedient. But this task her father set upon her shoulders was too much for her and she was so inexperienced.

"You will have to try. Nothing will happen. Besides, you must trust your father. He knows what is best and would not send you into danger." She tried to assure her.

"I would rather not leave home. I am scared."

"I am scared too," Thessalonike admitted. "I don't know what is going to happen to me—I have been betrothed twice already. At least you are getting the chance to start a life for yourself." She spoke the words to be encouraging and to try to help Nicaea to see the positive side of things, but her friend only cried more.

It was an hour before the tears had dried up and Nicaea had composed herself enough to apologize for her behavior.

"I am sure you are right." She smiled. "I shall try to be happy. For you." Then she stood and excused herself to get ready for dinner that night.

Thessalonike was worried for her friend.

The next time she saw Olympias, she mentioned it in passing.

"What is Antipater plotting?" Olympias was quick to suspect something amiss.

"Nothing. He just wishes to silence Perdiccas's ambitions. I am concerned about Nicaea. Perhaps you can convince him to not send her. I have never seen her so unhappy before."

But already Olympias's face was pondering the next move she would take. She placed a kiss on Thessalonike's brow and assured her all would be well before thanking her for the news.

Thessalonike gulped. She had a sense of uneasiness, but she tried to swallow it down. Nicaea was innocent, whatever her mother was plotting.

❧

Pella, 322 BC

Antipater had called her into the throne room. He was alone save for the guards at the door.

She looked at him expectantly. She supposed he had some marriage proposal for her or would ask her to host a banquet. So she was surprised to see the fury in his eyes as he regarded her.

"Care to explain why my daughter has been shamed and divorced in favor of your sister?"

"What?" Thessalonike was shocked.

"She is being sent home. Perdiccas seems to seek an alliance with your sister. After years of avoiding proposals, why has she suddenly agreed to this one?"

Thessalonike gulped. There was only one answer: Olympias.

"I did not know," she said firmly. "I am very sorry to hear of it and shocked. I am her friend."

"You've been a poor friend to her," he accused. He looked as though he was about to say something else, but instead he sent her away with a flick of his wrist.

Just months before, Antipater had returned victorious from putting down another Athenian rebellion. He had worked magic and proved himself an able general, just as he had been for Alexander. But now he was rewarded for his skill with an insult.

Curse you, Cleopatra, Thessalonike thought in her head. What was her conniving sister plotting? Olympias was sure that her daughter was under her control, but Thessalonike knew how Cleopatra craved power for herself. Had she jumped on this chance to gain power for herself or at the behest of her mother?

Thessalonike would bet on the latter.

❀

Pella, 321 BC

Everything was a disaster.

It did not help that she had sensed this coming since the news of Alexander's death had reached them. She had mourned for her brother, but she had also mourned for the fragile peace that was about to shatter as a result.

There had always been time. He was young. Heirs would come in time—he had not been worried. Of course, life never played out the way you wanted it to. Now his infant son was being pulled from one side to another, used as a mere pawn.

Antipater had marched on Perdiccas with the help of Craterus and his army.

By the time Antipater had reached Syria, there was barely a battle to be fought. The story had been that his own men had turned their swords on Perdiccas and murdered him.

Unfortunately, Craterus did not have the same luck. He

fought bravely at Hellespont, but a charging horse had ended his life.

Thessalonike remembered the kind man—even at the age of forty-nine he had been a strong rough man, but she had seen him with his wife and children too. He had been transformed by their presence. Thessalonike sighed, ticking off another death in her head. How many more people would die?

Olympias was strangely silent when she heard the news that Perdiccas had died. Her daughter was a widow once again, but this time it was hardly likely that she would be welcomed back home to Macedonia. Not when Antipater still harbored a grudge.

The one good thing to come out of this was that Nicaea was back in the palace. She stayed in a room close by Thessalonike, and the two women spent hours together.

"He was not a bad man." Nicaea reminisced about her brief marriage to Perdiccas. "I was not disappointed when he divorced me. I knew that my father would be mad, but I was glad to know that it meant I would be going home."

"Do you think he'll arrange another marriage for you?" Thessalonike asked.

"Perhaps, but he is occupied for now. Ever since he returned from Syria he has not been feeling well."

"I hope he gets better." Thessalonike looked away from her, picking up the gold thread to embroider into the red silk. There was more to this illness than the doctors thought, but she did not dare betray Olympias. She had picked her side, but she prayed to the gods that Olympias's latest ploy would fail.

Antipater had indeed not been feeling well since his

return, but that was likely more from exhaustion than anything else. His fever—that was Olympias's doing. It did not take much—just a drop or two in his food.

Thessalonike bit back the words she was going to say. It was too late now anyway. He would either survive or perish. She could admire Antipater for the skilled general he was, but otherwise she only cared because Nicaea loved her father so much. Even though he seemed to pass her around like a bargaining chip or reward.

Thessalonike moved the needle in and out of the cloth with expertise.

No one was safe. Not until there was a strong king on the throne.

Indeed, Nicaea was not with her for much longer. Antipater, who had made a miraculous recovery, had found another advantageous marriage for her to make. This time it was to Lysimachus, who was the governor of Thrace. This time she shed no tears as she prepared to leave for her new life. Thessalonike held her and gave her the red silk she had worked on herself as a wedding gift.

"Be safe."

With her departure, Thessalonike was alone once more save for the silent Olympias.

🐚

Pella, 319 BC

Within a week of his return from the fighting against those who had supported Perdiccas, Antipater was dead. This time his illness was brought on by natural causes, not Olympias's machinations. He received a lavish funeral and was given all the honors a man of his rank and status should get. Thessalonike had comforted Nicaea and her other sisters with patience, but inside she felt as though her heart had withered away to nothing.

She had known he was poisoned but did nothing. She glanced at Olympias, who out of respect attended the funeral too. She should be more like her—a stone statue, willing to cut down anyone who stood in her path.

What would happen to Macedonia now though?

The answer had shocked the council. As per Antipater's last instructions Polyperchon, an elderly Macedonian general who had served under her father Phillip and her brother, was appointed regent and commander of the empire.

Cassander had been overlooked. She had spotted him briefly at the funeral before he had conspicuously disappeared. She had recognized him by his hair. It was closer to auburn in color, but in the light of the pyre it had seemed to glow red. An ominous sign, in her opinion.

Olympias, meanwhile, seemed unconcerned about the new regent. He respected her and gave her a wide berth. They had developed an almost amicable relationship, but the steady peace at court would not last.

❀

Aigai, 319 BC

Cassander had not been fine sitting back to stew in his disappointment. He was a man of action. He went to his allies and with their help brought war down upon Macedonia.

His goal was to place Phillip III and Eurydice on the throne, driving Polyperchon out.

His initial attack was successful, and Polyperchon fled to Epirus with Roxana and her child.

The country was divided. Was the rightful ruler Alexander's son or his simple half-brother?

Thessalonike lived on a knife's edge for days as Olympias seemed to skitter about the old fortress deciding what she was going to do. If Cassander wished to become regent she could not blame him, but what she didn't like was that he seemed in no hurry to support Alexander's son.

It became apparent that he wished to use Phillip as a puppet king.

So in the dead of night Olympias fled, Thessalonike at her side, to Epirus and to war.

Thessalonike could not help the panic she felt. At night, she could not close her eyes from fear. During the day, she jumped at every little sound. She had become immobilized by the uncertainty.

She grasped at the strings of her support network that was no longer there. Maro was dead, Aya gone, Phila married to Antigonus's son, and Nicaea in Thrace. She felt alone.

"You should not trouble yourself with such dark thoughts," Olympias told her one night as she stroked her hair as though she were a child once more. "We shall be victorious. The priests have read the entrails, and they show victory."

Thessalonike did not dare voice her doubts. The priests could always be wrong. They had been in the past.

"Perhaps we shall arrange a marriage for you. Maybe with Antigonus?"

Thessalonike froze. Hadn't he sided with Cassander? Wasn't he too old?

"It is late. Think it over." She left Thessalonike with her thoughts. The girl had always been quick to fall into these depressions at stressful times like these, but it was time to fight now.

❧ 7 ❧

Pydna, 316 BC

At first they had won. Cassander was banished from Macedonia, and it seemed like Olympias was poised to take control.

The Macedonian army supported the mother of their deceased ruler. More importantly, they supported the son of Alexander, who they saw as the rightful king. Besides, Phillip III was not an attractive alternative.

Once Phillip's armies had been defeated, he had been captured along with Eurydice. Thessalonike had not seen them before they were dispatched. Once again she was not surprised by this terrible news. Her family tree dwindled once again. In her notes, she wrote down the dates of their death and wrote war as the cause.

It seemed that Olympias had finally succeeded, but before she could consolidate power, Cassander pushed back.

Now they had fortified themselves at Pydna as their armies prepared to wage war again.

"We can withstand a siege in here for years," Olympias assured both Roxana and Thessalonike, who followed after her through the narrow halls. "We shall win, but it is best to take a strategic position."

Roxana was quick to believe her, but still she feared for her seven-year-old son. Every day she thanked the gods he was still alive and well. Ever since the death of his father, she had wondered how long her precious child would live. He was still so young, but slowly, as one year had turned into seven, she had begun hoping that he might live to take his throne.

Under Olympias's assurance, she too began to be certain of his divine right.

Only Thessalonike remained skeptical, but she kept this to herself. She had cast her lot in with Olympias and she would not spread negativity now. What good would it do? Olympias would likely throw her from the parapets.

She thought of Europa, who had been a little child again. The faces and images of her family dead at the hands of her adoptive mother haunted her. She struggled with the love and sense of loyalty she felt toward her and the disgust.

Try as she might, she could not shake the deaths. It was as though she had taken the responsibility for them on herself. Olympias did not seem to care or be affected, though once or twice she had mentioned how it seemed every time she cut down an enemy, two appeared in their place.

"So stop cutting," Thessalonike had wanted to shout

but bit her cheek instead. It was better to stay on her good side.

She spent several quiet weeks inside Pydna before a messenger came running inside the walls shouting for the gates to be closed.

Cassander's army was on his heels. They had come after Polyperchon had fled with his men to some distant land.

Thessalonike's heart seized in terror at the thought of what would come next. Hunger and warfare. There was no time for escape and regrouping.

She would be trapped here, and she knew who had the upper hand in this case.

"You cannot do it. Do not trust him," Thessalonike urged Olympias, who shot a glare at her. Both women were gaunt with stress and hunger. It had been nearly two years since the siege had begun in earnest.

Now Cassander and Olympias had been negotiating peace and surrender. She bargained for her life, but Thessalonike did not think he would hold up his end of the bargain. She also noted dryly that Olympias had only arranged for her own safe passage and not that of Roxana and Alexander's precious son.

"Of course he won't touch you," Olympias had assured her, but Thessalonike did not believe her.

"Do not open the doors to him." She usually did not openly disagree with Olympias, but now was not the time for politeness.

The decision was made however, and there was no stopping her. Even Roxana was nervous. She shut herself in her room, clutching at Alexander and praying aloud in a language foreign to Thessalonike. But she could not find much pity for the woman who, much like Olympias, had slain her enemies. She had blood on her hands, but her seven-year-old son was innocent—perhaps the gods would spare him for the greater destiny that Olympias had foreseen for him.

Three days passed before the official surrender.

She stood on the parapet and watched as Olympias opened the gates to Cassander and surrendered to him.

She watched as Cassander accepted the surrender but then not a moment later ordered his soldiers to cut her down. Olympias remained frozen in place, but the soldiers refused to kill the mother of Alexander. They cried for mercy.

Cassander silenced them and raised his hand to speak again. Thessalonike bent forward, trying to catch what he was saying. Olympias was dragged off, and Thessalonike gave a cry before ducking down out of sight. It was too late—Cassander had caught sight of her dark blue chiton.

His soldiers stormed the fortress—they imprisoned those they found. Roxana and Alexander were dragged before Cassander.

They knelt before him, and Cassander promised them safety even as Olympias was being put to death by her enemies.

Thessalonike had been half dragged down from the parapets by soldiers. They were as gentle as they could be, but she was fighting the urge to faint.

"Be strong," she whispered under her breath.

Cassander spared her a glance before turning to the rest of the gathered people shifting uncomfortably before him. Days ago they had been enemies. Would he have them killed?

But Cassander promised in a loud voice that echoed across the fortress's courtyard that all would be treated well according to their station. They had been misled by Olympias and her plotting with Polyperchon. The deaths of Phillip III and his wife had been tragic murders. Olympias was a murderous traitor and had to be punished for her crimes.

Thessalonike regarded him with cold impassive eyes— why should she trust his words? After all, he had sworn that he would allow Olympias to live. Where was she now? It made Thessalonike sick picturing the fate her adopted mother had faced. Yes, she had not always agreed with her. Yes, she had committed some unforgivable acts, but she had raised and cared for Thessalonike. If it weren't for her, she would have fallen into obscurity. She did not hear the rest of what Cassander said to his men—it did not matter.

She needed to focus on survival for now.

Then the speech was over.

The fortress overrun with men loyal to Cassander no longer felt like the home she had lived in for the last few years. Thessalonike was led to her rooms by two guards, who stationed themselves outside her doors.

It was not the first time that she sat on her bed shaking, trying to calm her nerves, nor would it be the last. She felt so alone. But then she remembered that these guards did not know the secret passages of the fortress. Slipping through the back door of her private study, she managed to get to the courtyard without being stopped.

She was sitting on a bench catching a breath of fresh air when Olympias's body was carried past.

Her breath caught in her throat when she saw the bloodied body on the stretcher carried by two slaves. She couldn't tear her eyes away from the limp hand that peeked out from beneath the white linen cloth already stained red.

That hand had helped steady her as she learned to walk. It had helped teach her how to fix her hair, how to hold a shuttle at the loom.

Now it lay there unmoving.

The plain silver band was still on her finger. The slaves had not bothered removing the simple band—perhaps they were worried it contained some sort of spell as the symbol of the Dionysus cult.

But why were they carrying her off out the front gates? Wasn't she going to get a proper burial? No one looked too concerned as the mother of the king who had conquered the known world was carried off to get a pauper's funeral.

Thessalonike regarded the soldiers with disgust. It felt as if just moments ago they had refused to lay a hand on Olympias, but now it was as if she was utterly forgotten.

A sudden desire to escape filled Thessalonike.

She leaped to her feet and ran through the opened front gates, not looking back to see if anyone had seen her. They didn't pay too much attention to her. They were busy tending to other matters. They probably thought she was an errant slave girl running away.

As she ran, the ribbon that kept her hair tied up came loose and her hair flowed freely.

Thessalonike ran and ran until she found herself at the edge of the cliff overlooking the sea.

The crashing waves that had always terrified her looked inviting now. She wanted the fear to end. She wanted to escape. Perhaps this would be the noble way to do it. She remembered the bloodstained sheet covering Olympias. Perhaps this was the easiest way to go.

She heard a shout coming from behind her. The time for thinking was over.

And she took the plunge. The gods would forgive her.

❦

Cassander was out inspecting the camp and siege equipment being taken apart. A sense of accomplishment filled him as it always did after a victory. Finally, he would be the undisputed ruler of Macedonia, though he would be unable to call himself king officially.

There was still the problem of Roxana and her child, but he could deal with that in time.

Now he walked among his men, greeting a few he recognized, when a man shouted to a woman to watch out.

The woman ran through the camp like a crazed animal. He wouldn't have paid much attention to her, but he caught the glint of the circlet on her head and the dark navy gown he thought he recognized.

He frowned. Could it be her? He thought he had her taken to her rooms. He began following after her.

She was heading to the sea. His frown deepened and his steps hurried. His assistant dogged his steps.

"Where are you going, my lord?" Then he spotted the woman too. Her dark chiton fluttering in the wind as she regarded the sea below.

She was standing at the edge of a cliff—ready to jump.

Cassander called out to her to step away, but the woman was disobedient and took the last two steps necessary to fall into the watery depths below.

He rushed forward. The cliff was not too high, nor was the tide dangerous, but it was evident the woman could not swim or would not. He thrust his sword in his assistant's hands and in an instant dove down after her.

Cassander thanked his lucky stars that the sea had been relatively calm as he struggled to swim to shore. The unconscious woman was making his task all the more difficult.

His legs were weak as he pulled them up on the sandy shore and tried to awaken her. She might have taken in water and her pulse was weakening. He breathed life into her as he had been taught, and water came spurting out of her mouth. She choked, coughing violently, and then was alert again. Her pupils wide in fear.

When her gaze fell on him, she rasped out a weak curse.

"You should be more grateful." His own voice sounded exhausted, but his heart was beating fast from the adrenaline.

When he looked down at her again, it seemed as though she had fainted. No doubt from the shock.

His assistant came running down the beach. "Are you all right, sir?" he called.

"Yes." Cassander stood, his mind already listing off what he would have to do first. A bath and change of clothes before the feast tonight, then speaking to his generals, and tomorrow he could finish overseeing his camp... His thoughts trailed off as he looked at Thessalonike's pale face. With her dark hair fanned out in the sand and her willowy frame, she could be mistaken for a water nymph. Truly, she resembled a princess through and through. He thought idly that she was now the last princess of Alexander's line. She had become a precious commodity.

"We shall head back to the fortress. Who was set to watch her?" He frowned. One thing he hated was incompetence.

"I shall find out, milord." The assistant was still not sure who this woman was, but she was clearly important.

Cassander carried her back himself. They must have been quite a sight as they walked past his men and entered the gates.

A few servants rushed forward to take her off his hands, and he eagerly let them take her to see a doctor and to get looked after. "Take good care of her," he warned them before heading off to the bathhouse.

Thessalonike awoke in her room and she wondered if the cold waves had been a dream. The salty taste in her mouth reminded her that it had been no dream. She had taken that leap, but she had failed.

She could picture his face, red with effort on that nameless beach, and wondered why he had saved her. She shivered, feeling cold despite the blankets piled on her.

She turned her head to look around the room. Thessalonike did not recognize the maidservant who sat on a stool at her side. The girl was dozing off. Suddenly, she felt exhaustion hit her again, and she allowed herself to fall asleep again.

The doctors struggled for two days to keep the fever at bay. She fell in and out of sleep sporadically and she could not remember much.

Cassander had spared a few minutes to visit her and discuss her condition with her caregivers. She could hear them talking about her but could not respond.

"She has gone through a severe amount of stress. The water in her lungs is out now and her humors should be balancing out again," a doctor murmured in a learned tone.

"Do you think she has gone mad?" Cassander's blunt voice asked.

"No, once the fever has passed she should return to normal in no time," the doctor assured him, but in truth he had no idea himself. After all, she had thrown herself off a cliff. But it might have been her fear of Cassander's arrival that drove her to take that step forward. He had consulted with the servants who had served her in the past and they knew that she could not swim—she was afraid of water, apparently. This might all be a misunderstanding, but they would wait to see once she awoke.

Roxana was also allowed to visit her sister-in-law and spent some time by her bedside. She talked to her still form, urging her to get better and recover.

The doctor had asked if there was anything that might help her. Cassander had made it the doctor's top priority to see that the girl recovered. He didn't want to fail and face his wrath.

"She did have a companion, a slave girl she had freed that she was very close with. If anything, that girl would be instrumental in helping her recover," Roxana suggested, remembering Aya and how forlorn Thessalonike had been after her departure.

"Where is she?"

"She is living in a small city outside of Aigai. Her name is Aya and she is married to a butcher. Or a blacksmith." Roxana shrugged. She couldn't be sure.

"I shall have someone send for her."

By the time Aya arrived at Pydna, Thessalonike had awoken and was well enough to sit up on her own. She still had a terrible cough, as if she was still struggling to cough up the water she had inhaled. The doctors had warned her to watch out for infection caused by her tumble. Now her room was kept hot with braziers burning night and day.

Thessalonike had been shocked when her old friend stepped into the room with a two-year-old in tow.

"He's a handful." Aya ran her fingers through his dark hair. She sat by her friend's side after the introductions had been made.

"You can leave whenever you want." Thessalonike jumped in. "They should not have bothered you. I freed you."

"I came for my friend." Aya would have been insulted, but she saw how ill Thessalonike was and did not rebuke her or take her words to heart.

"Do they think I am crazy?" Thessalonike finally asked after she had Aya tell her all that had passed since they had last seen each other.

"I think the doctor is intent on declaring you are cured. He probably prays you have not gone mad." Aya gave a weary smile. "So now it is time for you to talk. Will you try to take your life again?"

Thessalonike was taken aback by the question. She thought for a moment before giving an honest answer. "No."

The voice in her head was gone. The hollow silence had disappeared. She felt strangely calm, and she surrendered herself to it.

"I am glad to hear that."

Aya took over caring for Thessalonike. Her son was a welcome addition to her rooms, filling them with the mindless babble of a toddler and squealing laughter. Thessalonike seemed to brighten when holding or playing with him.

It was two weeks before the trio were left alone. The doctors and other maids were dismissed and Thessalonike was declared cured, though she still stayed in her rooms most of the time.

"The fighting seems to have ended. Perhaps we can have peace." Aya looked as though she wanted this to be true.

"There are no longer any opposing factions. At least, none that I am aware of. I don't know what will happen to me, though. I also wonder what will be done with Roxana and her son," she admitted.

She had not been locked up, but she did not feel completely safe either. After all, Cassander could change his mind whenever he wanted. She was in his power. For now.

It seemed as though Cassander was debating what to do with the ragtag remainders of Alexander's family as well.

In the meantime, despite her recovery, Thessalonike had developed dark circles under her eyes. She had trouble falling asleep—all she could think about was daggers in the dark. She thought she had matured, but it seemed like her childhood dreams would continue to haunt her forever.

One day, a man entered her rooms. She vaguely remembered seeing him standing behind Cassander in the courtyard as he made his announcement.

Seeing her frozen at her desk, he bowed, surprising her by showing her the respect she was due.

"My lady, I have received instructions that I am to escort you back to Pella."

"What of my sister-in-law and her son?" She tried to keep her voice monotone.

He looked away for a brief moment, but she caught it. "They will not be joining you." He paused, as if unsure if he should tell her. "They will be placed under guard in Amphipolis."

She wanted to question him more but saw that she was already pushing her luck.

"Very well. When shall we leave?"

"I am arranging a retinue to leave in about three days. If that is acceptable?"

She gave him a nod and he left her rooms. What was she supposed to understand from this? She wondered why she was being separated from Roxana, not that she would miss her, but she was concerned for her nephew.

The next day she went to Roxana's rooms, where she was given permission to enter. Roxana presented a tough exterior, but Thessalonike noted the way she clutched at her son's hand possessively as though he was in the throes of a deadly illness.

In the rooms were two maids who she had never seen before. They must be spies. Roxana's own servants had been sent away a long time ago.

Did Cassander fear a conspiracy or that they would somehow find a way for Roxana to escape? There was no place for them to go, and the army that had followed behind Olympias would not rise up for her. They harbored a deep resentment toward her. They saw Roxana merely as the enemy. Only their respect for Alexander had protected her and what they saw as their duty to Alexander's son. Would they fight for him against their own countrymen? Not likely. Especially when he was still only a boy.

"Are you coming with us? They are taking us to the middle of nowhere," Roxana complained loudly, shifting her eyes to the silent maids.

"Amphipolis is a great city—a naval base." Roxana's eyes flickered with hope, but then she realized that it would likely mean she would be under close scrutiny.

"How is Alexander?" Thessalonike switched the topic and regarded the young boy clutching at a wooden soldier in his free hand.

"He is doing well and growing strong." Roxana put a hand on his head. As all young boys did, he tried to shake off his mother, not wanting to appear weak or childish.

"Is..." Thessalonike paused, unsure how to phrase the delicate question. "Does he have a tutor?"

Roxana gave her a thin smile and looked over her shoulder at the maids again. "They promise me he will have the best teachers arranged for him in Amphipolis. I do not trust them."

Thessalonike shifted uncomfortably then stood and began making her excuses to leave when there was a knock at the door.

It took all her will to keep herself from trembling as her enemy walked in.

Cassander was surprised to see Thessalonike in the rooms, but he greeted her with a smile, which she thought looked sly.

"I am glad to see you have improved."

"Improved?"

"They told me you were still sick after your fever and stayed confined to your room." He was looking past her, his gaze fixated on Roxana. "I expect to see you at dinner tonight," he added with finality in his voice, and she did not argue.

Thessalonike was unsure what to do, so she bowed and left the room. She wondered what he had to say to Roxana but knew that she had been dismissed.

She supposed she should attend dinner. Perhaps she would be able to gather some information, and she was going mad staying locked up in her rooms. She was glad she would have Aya by her side, though she would have to leave soon.

As night fell she allowed the maids to arrange her hair and dress her in a new gown. She picked a light gray one and pinned the material back with gold pins in the shape of the Vergina Sun. It was one of her more modest dresses, but she did not wish to catch anyone's attention while still wearing something appropriate for her rank.

The room fell silent as she entered. Thessalonike had not been expecting this. Cassander studied her for a moment before smiling and motioning for her to share his couch. A place of honor.

Just like that the tension in the room dissipated and conversations resumed, filling the room with chatter.

She approached him as if he was an angry guard dog. Moving slowly and taking deliberate steps. She did not avoid his gaze but matched it with one of her own. The important thing was to show no fear, she heard Olympias say in her mind.

So she sat beside him with a smile and accepted a cup of honeyed wine.

He regarded her with admiration at the composure she showed. Still, he treated her as if she was a skittish horse ready to run or bite at the slightest provocation. There had to be peace, and he would do his best to safeguard her. A decision had been made in the back of his mind, but he would not say anything for now. There was plenty of time in the future.

"May I ask why you are sending me to Pella?" Her voice interrupted his trail of thoughts.

"I thought you would be more comfortable." He looked perturbed by her question, as though he wondered why she even needed to ask the question. "You would be the first lady of the city now."

The idea did not seem to please her, and she set down her cup to hide the tremor of her hand. He remembered that Olympias had once been the first lady.

"My sisters are all married and away from court, but the capital needs a strong presence while I will be away." He changed the topic. "I know you were close friends with my sister Nicaea."

"I have not seen her for several years, but we were close." She kept her response distant, almost suspicious of his friendly behavior toward her. Why was he being so open? She did not see Roxana at this banquet and she had just as much rank as Thessalonike, if not more.

"She is thriving in Thrace—she has had a son. I am sure she would wish to hear from you." He was not lying. His sister had written to him to inquire after Thessalonike.

"And what do you plan to do now?" Thessalonike put on her politician's face.

"I have business in the south." He was being standoff-ish, as though he feared admitting his plan to this snipe of a woman. The way she smiled up at him from her seat made him wonder if she could read his mind. So after a moment he went on.

"I plan to restore Thebes and consolidate my power over the rest of the city-states."

Thessalonike was shocked, and she did not bother hiding it. "Thebes? That would take several years."

His lips were set in a grim but determined line. "It will be restored."

"People might accuse you of snubbing my brother." She did not bother being politically correct and careful with her words. The cup of wine was being refilled in her hands. Her attitude had shifted to that of a deft politician.

"It is an important city," he replied coolly but was intrigued by the way she had changed.

"Was." She grinned up at him and drank greedily from the cup in her hands.

Let's see what you can do, she challenged silently.

❦

Pella, 312 BC

Thessalonike was admiring the bracelet Cassander had sent to her. It was her prize.

She had bet him that Seleucus and Ptolemy would defeat Antigonus's son Demetrius. It had been a foolish bet, seeing as the odds were against her. Demetrius had the superior army, but she had trusted in Seleucus's cleverness.

From what people were saying, it was evident that he had been able to surprise Demetrius and cut his army to shreds. Demetrius had even been captured but quickly released. Antigonus had become quite powerful and consequently was now Cassander's greatest enemy.

She put on the gold bracelet with the ruby jewel encrusted at the center with a sense of pride.

Winning was addictive. She supposed she was doomed to suffer from this fault ever since her father had named her Victory in Thessaly.

It had been four years since the siege at Pydna. Four long years.

So much had changed.

Her bulging stomach was one piece of undeniable evidence. The gods had been kind and had already given her two children named Phillip and Antipater. At her age, she was considered old to have any children, but Cassander had always been certain their marriage would be fruitful.

Thessalonike still thought of the last time she had the astrologers predict her future. The crown had come to her when Cassander had married her, and now it seemed the children would follow too. She would have three, if the astrologer was to be believed.

After she had been sent back to Pella, she had happily returned to her old routine. The servants and officials of the city tiptoed around her for a while, but she showed them that all was well. As Cassander instructed, she held banquets and oversaw feasts. Just like before, she was kept in the public eye, and the people seemed to admire her for her steadfastness. It was a time of change and unrest for everyone.

The Diadochi, Alexander's great generals, were still

vying for control, even though his kingdom had been split up.

His last words haunted them like a curse and premonition. "Let the strongest inherit."

Thessalonike smiled. Did he even know what he had said or what his words would lead to? Regardless, men were addicted to fighting. She doubted even if he had named a successor that there would be peace. They would have torn the man up like a pack of wild dogs.

Cassander had been true to his word. Roxana remained unharmed, though confined in the great naval city Amphipolis, and her son was thriving. He was nearing his majority when he would be claiming his crown. Perhaps then he could perform some magic and bring the fighting to a standstill.

At least in Macedonia. Thessalonike touched her belly again.

Cassander had returned a year after going to rebuild Thebes. She had seen to it that he and the army were greeted with the pomp and celebrations that were necessary. He had seemed pleased with her but had still walked on eggshells around her for days.

It was when he had invited her to walk with him in the courtyard that she knew what was coming. This was something she had suspected for some time, but she thought perhaps there were things holding him back such as her age. She had been thirty-six when he declared his intention to marry her. He had done it first in a private place, as though he feared her reaction.

She had been guarded, but she had agreed. After all, this would be the best and safest thing for her to do.

There could be worse options, and though she would

never forget that he had ordered Olympias's death, she supposed she could come to forgive him. No one was innocent in this world.

Especially not Olympias, who had cut down her enemies ruthlessly.

The courtiers and generals had gossiped that Thessalonike was an old dried-up spinster, but here she was three years later, nearly ready to deliver her third baby.

The news had shocked Cassander, who for once had been truly jubilant over the news.

She would never forget the gleam in his eyes after she had told him she was carrying his first child.

He had not taken another concubine or wife since marrying her. Not that he had time to do so between border skirmishes and dealing with the city-states. She was positive he had his dalliances on the side, but she was secretly happy she did not have to share her position with another. Nor would her children be threatened by a rival.

She touched her belly again, picturing the child growing inside of her. She was certain it would be a boy again.

As Thessalonike was preparing for the birth of her third child, Fortuna was busy spinning her wheel.

Thessalonica, 310 BC

Cassander was by her side as he showed her the new palace that was nearly finished being constructed. Thessalonica was named after her and promised to be one of Cassander's greatest projects. Surrounding the city were

ANNE R BAILEY

over twenty villages, and the strategic position would ensure Thessalonica became a power base that could one day replace Pella.

"You shall decorate it however you see fit," Cassander announced.

"Was there any question about that?" She grinned, already planning what to do with each room they passed through. They came to the royal apartments and she picked the perfect one for Phillip. His rooms overlooked the inner courtyard where she had planted fruit trees. It would be perfect for him. Their oldest son was now five years old, while their youngest was finally starting to walk.

There was no doubt in her mind that they had been blessed.

Cassander in turn honored her by naming this city after her.

She knew things were not sitting so well with him. The council had decreed that once Alexander IV came of age, he would be crowned king of Macedonia. The peace treaty they had drawn up just a year before had fallen into ruins for the most part.

Antigonus had placed troops in the supposed free Greek city-states, and that gave Cassander and Ptolemy the excuse to rise up against him too.

Cassander was the commander of all of Europe, with Antigonus as his counterpart in Asia Minor—it was a recipe for disaster of course. Each man was unsatisfied with what they had and they bickered constantly. Their fights usually turned into outright skirmishes and wars.

Cassander had married her to align himself with the Argead dynasty—Alexander's dynasty. His young son was the nephew of the long-dead king. She was not naïve enough to think that he had married her for love. Still, it irked her the way he liked to throw around her heritage. He respected her and treated her kindly, but in public he used her as a political tool.

This was something that she barely tolerated.

Antigonus continued to be a plague upon him. As a proper wife, she should have hated him too, but in a way she felt that Cassander deserved this little test. After all, hadn't he opposed and chased off the last regent too?

He should be kept on his toes. As she thought this, she leaned up and placed a kiss on his cheek.

"You are planning to make sure I don't have a moment's peace."

"There is no rest for the wicked," he teased, but she did not appreciate the comment and pulled away. Perhaps he knew her better than she thought.

Sometimes he would chide her for what he called impertinence.

"What secrets are you hiding behind that pretty smile of yours?" he asked one night as he lay by her side.

"What makes you think I keep secrets from you?" She had pushed him away, but he had strengthened his hold on her waist.

"I see you whispering to people. I know you've been in Pella longer than I have. This is your world, not mine." He voiced his fears.

She merely kissed his nose and declared he was being paranoid.

He was in fact paranoid. He did not like being reminded of her great heritage and family. The royal blood that flowed in her veins was both a curse and a boon in his eyes.

Thessalonike watched him until he fell asleep. She knew he hated meddling women, so she had strived to cultivate the image of a supportive woman for him. She did not want him to accuse her of being a witch or unfit wife.

Unlike Olympias, who had a powerful family at her back, Thessalonike had no one. She could not openly plot, but for now she had no desire to do that either. She'd seen how destructive that tendency could be. She swore she would try to go no farther than what her duty required her to do.

They returned to Pella the next day and she coddled her young sons. Before she knew it they would be too old to be petted and held in her arms. Soon they would have to be sent away to be tutored in the arts of war and politics.

❧ 8 ❧

Pella, 309 BC

Thessalonike often invited Aya to stay with them at court. She had gone from servant to companion.

Thanks to her old mistress, her husband was awarded a post in the city that paid well, and they were able to keep a modest house of their own. They had managed to find an apprenticeship for her son as a scribe. It was her greatest wish for him to become a great scholar rather than a soldier. Aya harbored a great fear of her child dying in battle, especially since she only had her one son.

Thessalonike welcomed her warmly and invited her to sit by the fire.

It was winter and a chill had descended on the palace.

They talked for a long time, exchanging pleasantries from the latest fashions to the weather. Aya wondered what Thessalonike was hiding now. Usually she was much more open and exuberant when she saw her.

Then she noted the circles under her eyes and the way

she pushed away the little appetizers the servants served the pair of gossiping women.

"Do you have news for me?" Aya finally dared to ask when there was a break in conversation.

"What do you mean?" Thessalonike tried to look innocent.

"I suspect you are with child again."

"Hush." She put a finger to her lips. She didn't want the others overhearing and spreading the news. "It is true. I have missed my courses for two months now." She bit her lip. "Or it could be that I am no longer fertile."

"Nonsense. You have lost your appetite, haven't you?" Aya reassured her. "You should tell your husband soon. He'll order another celebration and all the merchants will profit. Maybe he'll commemorate it with a statue." Aya was hopeful for the work her husband might get.

"Now you are being ridiculous. People have babies all the time."

"Ah, but this will be his fourth child and it wouldn't be as special."

Thessalonike smiled. Yes, at least of that she could be certain. Even at her age, it seemed she was going to create a brood for Cassander.

She waited another week before approaching him. He had been spending far too much time locked up in his office with his generals, poring over maps and looking for ways to expand his empire.

She was content being left to manage her own affairs. She did not crave his company or constant attention, but she was anxious to share this news with him.

She came into the room on the heels of servants

carrying trays of food to replenish his strength, and she pulled him off to the side.

He regarded her with a tinge of annoyance in his eyes. He had been in the middle of drafting a treaty to send to Ptolemy against Antigonus.

"You don't need to look so put out, husband." She took his hand in hers. "I wanted you to know I am with child again." She did not bother skirting around the news and was rewarded by his grip tightening on her hand.

"You are?" He looked happy—that gleam in his eyes was back as he regarded her with a warmth he only reserved for special occasions.

She nodded and he kissed her temple. "I am very happy. You must take care of yourself. Order anything you like."

"Thank you, Cassander." She left him to his work.

Cassander was distracted after she left. He was starting a little dynasty of his own. It was not the first time he had thanked the gods for letting their paths cross. She had been a good wife—tending to the household, dealing with entertainments, and arranging social events. But she had also brought to him the connection with Alexander. Their sons were his descendants and after Alexander IV were the next in line for the throne. He had never played up this fact to his cohorts nor did he allude to it too much, but the reminder was in his head every time he saw his sons or held his wife.

The council had voted to instate Alexander IV to the throne in a few years. The child, who was being held at Amphipolis, was getting a good education—he had seen to it himself. He did not want people accusing him of making trouble or having designs on the throne.

He had to be seen as respectful of Alexander the Great's legacy.

Roxana was imprisoned for her own misbehavior. She was constantly trying to find a way to escape and dreamed of gathering an army to install her son on the throne. Regardless, no one liked or trusted her. They did not raise any objections to his treatment of her.

He had to tread a careful path with her son, though.

His father had always criticized him for reaching too high and letting ambition get in the way of doing what was right.

The throne seemed ever closer now, and it tempted him more and more with each passing year.

❀

Amphipolis, 309 BC

There was no peace for Roxana lately. The sweltering heat made every breath she took feel as though she was drowning. At night bugs and mosquitos buzzed around her.

She had finally begged to be let out. The walls of the room she was confined in seemed to be bearing down on her and she could no longer stand it.

It had been over a month since she had seen her son, and she feared that something had happened to him.

She hated Cassander. She hated everyone who came into her room and looked at her as if she was a crazy woman. Perhaps she was. She screamed out in frustration, hitting the door with her fists.

"Let me out!"

Roxana fell asleep by the door after exhausting herself.

The servants had to carry her to her bed and tried to groom her, but she awoke and lashed out at them.

"Where is my son?" Her voice seethed, full of hate.

"There is no need to concern yourself with him. He is well—you must let us look after you."

"No." She pulled away from the woman and crawled to the opposite edge of the bed. "Where is my son?" she repeated again.

The woman looked at the others and finally, shrugging, stood to leave the room.

The soldiers locked the door behind the women and Roxana was alone again, but at least she was safe. They couldn't poison her if she was alone. They couldn't attack her.

Somewhere in the depths of her mind where the old Roxana still lingered, the urge to cooperate came forth. If she behaved, she might be allowed out. But that was quickly replaced by fear and anger.

She knew that they were trying to separate her from her son. She would not be able to protect him here.

Where are you? She moved to the boarded-up window that let in only a couple streams of light. She tried to look out but could not see anything.

❦

Pella, 309 BC

Thessalonike was awoken by the sharp kick of the baby within her. He hardly let her rest. The dark circles under her eyes were deepening, and the doctors were worried she would be prone to illness if she did not get rest.

They crafted her potions to calm the baby down and soothe her. It was only in the bathhouse as she floated in the water that the baby seemed to calm down, but she was uncomfortable in the water. Memories of long ago still haunted her.

She felt uneasy and stood to walk around the empty corridors. She was a common sight to the soldiers on guard, and they saluted her as she passed.

She went to find Cassander but did not find him in his rooms. She did, however, find him asleep at his desk. The oil lamp had burned out long ago and she replaced it herself.

She was about to call for his manservant to help him get to his room when she spotted the papers on his desk. They were written with the meticulously precise handwriting she was so familiar with.

He was working on a family history, it seemed. Tracing his ancestry as far back as he could remember. This was a rough draft. As she moved past the recollection of Antipater's accomplishments, she came to Cassander. There among the victories he'd won and peace treaties he'd drawn up was their wedding date. Then, after the rebuilding of Thebes, was the birth of their son. She brushed a finger over his name. What a sweet boy he was. Then she continued scanning the document. There was the building of Thessalonica—a crowning achievement.

There were other battles and accounts, but what caught her eye was the last entry. Cassander — rightful ruler of Macedonia. It had been crossed out, but she feared what this meant. With a shaky hand, she set the document back down where she had found it and hoped he would not notice.

His breathing was still coming steadily, so she studied the other letters and papers on his desk. She riffled through a few of them as quietly as she could. Most were not relevant to what she was looking for, but then she found a report from Amphipolis. She read it as quickly as she could.

"Roxana has lost her wits. Attacks everyone who enters like a wild animal. She keeps asking for her son, but we don't trust her with him. She has tried to set her room on fire, but luckily we got there in time to stop her. Please advise on what should be done."

Thessalonike bit her lip. What had they done to Roxana to make her go insane? She had never had mad tendencies, nor would she do something as crazy as set fire to her own room. She was a vicious fighter but a smart woman.

A small snore from Cassander made her flinch, and she set down the letter and snuck out of the office quickly. It was better he didn't know she had come in.

The only thing standing between Cassander and claiming the throne was Roxana and her son, the rightful king. Ever since they had been sent away to Amphipolis, she had not brought up the question for fear of angering Cassander and opening up the discussion to uncomfortable topics. She knew that they were still alive and well, so she had never made further inquiries.

In the account books, she had seen payment go out for Alexander's tutors and instructors, so she had no reason to fear he was being held under terrible circumstances.

That letter painted a different picture. If mother and son were kept apart and Roxana was locked up, Cassander might be plotting something.

She had wanted to trust him, and indeed for six years

he had kept his promise that Roxana and Alexander would be safe. He could have had them executed on the day he conquered Pydna, but he had not and had treated them with every respect.

What had changed?

The answer hit her with some force as the truth was revealed to her. She had given birth to a healthy son and now she was pregnant again. Through her, Cassander had a legitimate claim to the throne. If Alexander was out of the way, then no one could object to him claiming the crown. It only made sense.

She shivered. Surely this was all in her head. Would he dare to commit such an unsavory act?

She was tired again and walked back to her rooms to try to get some rest.

🍂

Amphipolis, 209 BC

They were coming for her.

Roxana could hear them whispering in the hallway. She was ready for them. A sharp shard of glass was in her hand, ready to be used on any would-be assailants. Let them come.

They had moved her from the now-charred room she had lived in for the last seven years. The stark room she was in now was more of a dungeon than anything else. It was hardly suitable to house Alexander's queen. She called herself that now and demanded everyone do the same.

"I can hear you," she yelled from behind the thick wooden door. "I am the queen and I can hear everything."

The whispers stopped for a moment before resuming. She relished in the fear she was able to extract from them. Let them think she was crazy. She would find a way out of here and then they would all be sorry. She would cut their throats herself. She would relish the looks in their eyes as they took their last breaths knowing she was the cause of their demise.

For days, she dreamed of this and often called out to the slaves who came to give her food. They did not trust her with utensils anymore, and she ate with her hands as though she was a common peasant. They fed her crude bread, slop, and occasionally meat. This was not food fit for a queen, she would hiss at them, but she ate it anyway, seeing how hungry she was.

Then one day as she finished a rant she heard the key turning in its lock. She waited with anticipation, wondering if anyone would come in.

A man entered. She did not waste a moment and lunged forward, her crude weapon in hand.

She managed to slash his cheek before two hands pulled her away. She was held by two soldiers, who took her weapon from her and held her before the man.

He was frowning at her now. A hate as fierce as her own.

"You are a madwoman and a witch," he spat.

She merely smiled and was lost in her thoughts. She did not hear what he said next, but before she knew it she was being led out of the rooms.

She would be free, she thought gleefully. Free.

Then her world collapsed in front of her as she was brought to the back of the mighty fortress. A voice in her head told her to run—this was an execution ground. She struggled now, and the soldiers had a hard time holding on to her.

She spotted a figure on the ground. She squinted against the glare of the sun that her eyes were not adjusted to yet.

Slaves rushed forward to carry the unmoving body away. As they lifted the body, she recognized who it was from the thick curls on his head and let out a horrifying screech.

She was pushed forward by the soldiers and she stumbled. Roxana would have fallen to her knees if it wasn't for them holding her up.

She met her death with disbelief, cursing those around her. Promising to visit death upon their houses, before her world went dark.

❀

Pella, 309 BC

She screamed as the midwives urged her to push.

Maids were coming to and fro from the room, carrying pitchers of warmed water.

Aya sat by her side, replacing the cool compress on her forehead and whispering comforting words.

Thessalonike did not want comfort. She raged as she struggled to give birth to her latest child. Her mind was a vision of red as she thought of Roxana and her son—dead miles away. They had been buried without much fuss made over their coffins or tombs. A hasty burial to help them disappear quickly from the memories of the people.

"Cassander," she hissed as she felt another spasm take over her body.

"You are doing fine." Aya encouraged her over her screams.

She wanted him to pay for what he had done. One day soon. She cursed him over and over in her head. Let his plotting end in ruin.

Through gritted teeth she continued pushing and focused on the task at hand.

At last her son was born. He was a bawling baby, already kicking and screaming for all the world to hear.

The midwives wiped him down and washed him clean.

Thessalonike was exhausted. Her fury had abated, but as they held the baby up to her she could not manage much of a smile.

"Tell my husband," she murmured to Aya before falling asleep.

She slept through most of the day. The doctors had been called in, and they feared she suffered from a complication during the birth. What she wouldn't admit was that she had exhausted herself with the effort of her cursing.

"He wishes to call him Hector," Aya told her as she fed her from a bowl of warm stew.

"That's a good name."

Aya regarded her for a moment. Thessalonike was not usually so apathetic, especially not when it came to children.

She wondered if she was to blame. Thessalonike had taken the news of her nephew's death badly. Two days later she went into labor. Now Aya kept the information to herself that Polyperchon was raising an army with astonishing speed to put Hercules, the illegitimate son of Alexander, on the throne.

She would tell her later. For now, Thessalonike needed to recover her strength.

Thessalonike stood before him, her shoulders squared back. If he had been a weaker man, he would have been terrified by the intense rage and hatred with which she looked at him now.

"How can you negotiate with that man?"

"Do you have an army of over twenty thousand? If you do, I could use it now." He usually did not respond to her goading remarks, but he was angry too.

"You are weak," she hissed. "You are not a general. My brother fought the Persians and sent them running with half the army you have at your disposal. He fought a war when the treasury was nearly empty. Now it is full and you struggle. Are you scared of some illegitimate child?"

"You should do a better job at hiding your contempt for me. I am making a prudent decision. One that I do not have to discuss with you." He retreated back into his cool exterior, and she knew her comments had hit their mark.

She smirked.

"You are having trouble reaching an agreement with him." She was not guessing. She knew the man from his dealings with Olympias. She had been present as they sat debating for days about the terms of their arrangement. She had learned how his mind worked, but she doubted Cassander would or could comprehend this. "Money will mean nothing to him. If you have already plied him with money, then you have done nothing but insult him."

Cassander all but jumped to his feet. He worked hard to hold back his emotions.

"You should decide whose side you are on. You are married to me. You have sons with me. You should think of them." They were playing a game of tug-of-war. She was threatening to let him slide and fail, and he was threatening to take her down with him.

"You must give me more credit than that." She relented. "I just want you to remember who helped you win. I want you to remember," she repeated, approaching him.

She was no longer the skittish horse. She was a hunter who had just locked on to her prey. "I want you to thank me."

"And I shall once he is dealt with," Cassander conceded and wondered if she knew that at the moment he was trying to decide between kissing her and smashing her pretty little head against the wall.

The silence was deafening as they regarded each other. Studying each other for weaknesses.

Finally, she took a seat across from his desk—they were equals now.

Her advice had proven more valuable than Cassander wished to admit. Once the surprise had worn off, he regarded his wife with a new appreciation—there was a wealth of knowledge that he could tap.

In the end, Polyperchon was offered a position as a general in Cassander's own army as well as a governorship. He would be brought back into the fold of the great Diadochi rather than fighting against them. As an added bonus, Thessalonike had sent her own letter extolling her husband's virtues and begging him to put aside his differences with Cassander.

Her opinion counted for something as the legitimate

sister of Alexander. Olympias had raised her as her own daughter and he knew this. He held great respect for the old royal family, and in the end he conceded.

She was with Cassander when he received the news that Hercules had been assassinated at his request. She had hardened her heart to this reality of life. All pretenders needed to be destroyed.

She waited for several days for him to thank her. Had he forgotten who had helped him? Out of spite, she let it leak that he had ordered Hercules's assassination. Not that this was surprising in a day and age when everyone was busy killing the other, but the act was not seen as honorable. Hercules had not had a proper trial, nor had he died fighting. They would call Cassander a coward.

Thessalonike did not have to wait long for him to come storming into her rooms. She sent Antipater and his nurse out of the room and urged Phillip to leave as well.

Cassander waited until their children were out of the room before beginning his rampage. "You little snake. I suppose you are the one behind the latest rumors about me."

"They are true—aren't they? I warned you that we were going to work as partners from now on. You failed to uphold your end of the bargain."

He took a threatening step forward and she mimicked him. "You were supposed to thank me."

His hand, which had caressed her cheek at night, now seemed ready to strike, but she remained unmoved—as if she dared him to make a move.

"And how shall I thank you?" His voice was gruff.

"Will you kneel before me?" She stepped forward, and suddenly there was only a hair's width parting them.

"Never."

"Good." She wrapped her arms around him, pulling him into a searing kiss. Her fingernails digging into his back.

In the privacy of her room, he let her lead the way.

That afternoon she overpowered him. She commanded. She ruled.

As their passion cooled, they lay side by side, their eyes fixated on the ceiling.

"I appreciate your help." Cassander's voice finally broke the silence.

"I needed to hear you say it." Thessalonike shifted to look at him. "You are right. Our children are the future— they have bound us together and I will work to help you succeed." She trailed a hand down his bare chest. But I can also make things difficult for you, she added to herself, knowing he was aware of this as well.

"Look at them, Alexander." She held her youngest son in her lap, pointing to the brightly colored fish swimming in the pond. He laughed happily, reaching for them, and she gave him some food to throw to them. "You are my slippery little fish." She laughed with him as he tried to worm free to get a closer look at them.

The fish scattered as a rock landed in the middle of the pool. She pulled away from the water and looked around to see who had done that.

"Antipater, why did you do that?" She scowled at him. In her arms, Alexander was crying. His friends had gone and he had been startled by the rock.

"He's such a crybaby."

"You shall go to your rooms and stay there without dinner until tomorrow. If you continue misbehaving, I shall turn you over to your father." Her menacing threat sent him running.

She frowned, watching him go, and had a maid go watch him before turning back to her youngest.

"You cannot cry at every little thing, Alexander." She wiped his face with the edge of her chiton. "Promise you'll be my brave little soldier?"

He nodded and she put him down. His nursemaid would watch him while she went to scold Antipater. He was growing into a jealous and spiteful child, always getting into mischief. She had once blamed herself for not paying attention to him. Phillip, as his father's heir, received prominence. Alexander had always been sickly, requiring special attention, and now Hector had been born, so there was even less time for the independent Antipater.

Thessalonike had tried to ply Antipater with little gifts and even spent whole afternoons with him. She spoiled him with attention, but it still did not seem to be enough. Just last week she had caught him pinching Alexander while he slept in his crib. What scared her was that he seemed to enjoy making others cry.

She hoped she would be able to break him of whatever sick habit he had developed.

❀

Thessalonica, 307 BC

Thessalonike drummed her nails on Cassander's desk as he paced, reading the missive he'd received out loud.

"He was proclaimed Theoi Soteres. Divine hero. Along with his father." Cassander could not keep the contempt from his voice.

"I warned you the governor was a weak-minded fool. He abandoned his post at the first sign of trouble." She weighed in.

She had finally pushed herself forward. Ever since Hector had died just before his first birthday from a fever, she had been pushed into action. She no longer cowered behind her fear. She was no longer willing to allow others to decide her future. For once she would make her own path. There would be a price to pay, but she was fully aware of the dangers she took. She embraced it and used it to motivate herself.

This had been the dawn of a new era.

"What am I going to do?" He groaned, shoving the message off his desk. He would have burned it in rage, but he wanted to have a reminder.

"We shall have to content ourselves with Macedonia. The Greek city-states were never under the total control of neither my brother nor my father."

"You think I am not capable of maintaining control?"

She resisted the urge to roll her eyes. Sometimes he was just as needy as her children for attention and validation.

"There is no need for you to spread your resources too thinly. Once we have consolidated power here, then we can turn to expansion, but I still think Greece is the wrong place to try to conquer. Since the beginning of time, they have fought to maintain their independence. They have never truly unified, and even when they did it only lasted a few years. I think you are wasting your time." She spoke bluntly and usually he appreciated it, but tonight he was more annoyed than anything.

In the end, he agreed to wait. He did nothing more than bolster defenses and brood in his office at night.

Thessalonike knew what he wanted. He wanted to ride at the head of an army leading Macedonia to greatness as Alexander and her father had done. He was missing that spark in him, though.

Rather than trust him, men seemed weary around him. Cassander did not draw loyalty and inspiration from his men. He had to find other ways of getting what he wanted. Secretly, she was not surprised they felt this way.

After all, hadn't he openly usurped the throne? Hadn't he assassinated countless rivals? He was never the most popular or the noblest of Alexander's old generals, but she appreciated his meticulous ruthlessness.

She was watching Phillip in the courtyard as he played with Antipater, playing her lyre. Somewhere in the palace, the maids were coddling her youngest son Alexander. He had always been sick as a baby, and even now that he was five years old she feared he would catch a cold if he was outside too much.

However, Alexander made up for his weak constitution with a mouth that never seemed to cease talking.

Cassander, who was quite reserved with his own words, was horrified by his son's brashness.

"He's only a child." Thessalonike shrugged when he had expressed his concern.

A servant ran into the pavilion. He looked quite

winded, and she knew something important had happened.

"What is it?" She put her lyre aside.

"Your husband is looking for you, my lady."

She followed after him to the familiar offices where she usually found herself plotting with Cassander.

"Close the door and leave us," he ordered the servant as she entered.

"Husband?"

"Epirus has sided with Antigonus."

Her eyes widened. Frankly, she was surprised he was so calm.

"I thought they were our loyal allies. They have always been the allies of Macedonia."

Thessalonike coughed, wondering how to put this tactfully. "You killed our last connection to Epirus. The only reason they supported Macedonia was because of family ties to us."

Cassander's hand twitched in fury, mechanically reaching for the sword he kept at his side only to find it was not there.

"We are surrounded now. I should have pressed war with Demetrius when I had the chance."

She frowned. He had not said it out loud, but it was clear he was blaming her.

"I gave you sound advice. Our position is not weaker. What if you had engaged Demetrius and then Epirus swept in from the west? You need to—"

He slammed a fist on his desk. The reverberating noise stunned her into silence, then anger. If he was going to behave like a child, she wasn't about to entertain him, and she left the room without another word.

They did not speak for weeks, and then he declared war on Demetrius.

While he was raising his army and preparing for war, she seethed in her rooms, positive he would see she had been right.

🦁

Aigai, 303 BC

She welcomed Cassander back as any dutiful wife should. Their three sons were now standing behind her. It felt as if no time has passed since they had been babes – confined to their nursery, unable to walk, much less talk.

She watched as they greeted their father. She kept a close eye on Antipater, who enjoyed causing trouble. They performed their bows, still a little shaky, but it brought a smile to her face.

The servants led the children away, and Thessalonike retreated to speak with Cassander privately.

In public, she did not rebuke him, but in private her annoyance with him was made plain.

"We received word that Ptolemy's ships were destroyed. This leaves Antigonus with control of the Aegean Sea and half the Black Sea."

"You don't need to lecture me on things I already know."

"Don't I? Didn't I tell you to cement your lands here? Now your hard-won victories in Athens and Attica are for nothing." She did not relent.

Perhaps she should have been gentler with him. Plying

someone with honey always worked better than using vinegar.

"What do you suggest, wife?"

He had not meant for her to answer, but she pressed forward with an already-rehearsed speech. His best chance was to ally himself with Ptolemy.

Cassander knew this of course, but he was being as stubborn as a bull about it. She did not know the relationship between the men who had fought with Alexander, but she suspected there was an intense amount of competition and resentment mixed in with mutual respect. At least, they could ally together to defeat their common enemy. Now with his navy destroyed, Ptolemy was surely willing to come to the discussion table and broker an agreement.

Antigonus was gaining more and more land—soon he'd be unstoppable.

Cassander did not say anything as she finished but excused himself so he could go to the bathhouse. Tonight, after the appropriate sacrifices were made, they would feast.

Eventually, she had her answer. Cassander had indeed spoken with Ptolemy and they would soon join together as allies with Lysimachus. He had not said anything to her and in fact, she had to hear the news from her little spies she paid to report back to her.

But for a while, he had been attentive to her, and she knew that was his way of thanking her.

The days felt longer now—perhaps she was starting to show her age.

She had turned forty-five and the lines on her face and graying hair made her appear too old to have such young children.

Phillip had begun his training under tutors selected by Cassander and herself. He was doing well in both his combat training and other courses. He seemed to like mathematics the most. Her boy would grow up to be a brilliant strategist.

She found she always tried to be by his side as he learned or studied. Always reminding him of who he was and his heritage.

Cassander had accused her of trying to turn the child against him, but she would merely push him away. She liked maintaining a certain level of closeness with her children and prided herself in the love they showed her in return—except for Antipater, that is.

❀

Pella, 300 BC

Her efforts had paid off.

The man who had plagued her for years of worry and kept her husband constantly away fighting wars was now dead. Antigonus had perished a year ago, but his presence was still felt throughout Greece and Asia.

Thessalonike thought grimly of his son Demetrius, who had maintained a strong foothold in Greece. Perhaps they would never be rid of him. She studied the maps outlining their borders. He was in a strong position to move against Macedonia if he wanted to.

But for now, there was a shaky peace.

Cassander had finally thrown his full support behind Ptolemy and Lysimachus. Together the men had destroyed their common enemy. More importantly, as Thessalonike was always reminding Cassander, he had finally been acknowledged by the others as the rightful king. He had been crowned five years ago, but it was not until the death of Antigonus that this had been cemented.

After the disaster of temporarily losing Thessaly, she had flown into action, calling upon all her knowledge to try to turn the tides for her husband. It was always at the back of her mind that if he should fall before her children were old enough to defend themselves, then they would all perish.

The solution she had come up with had been something taken out of Olympias's book, except it was much less bloody.

Philetaerus was a Macedonian general who had risen to prominence under her brother. He had several legions under his control and by all accounts was as smart as he was skilled with his spear.

The fact that he had unfortunately sided with Antigonus could be remedied.

She had not told Cassander what she was planning, knowing he would disapprove. Though he had been suspicious when she locked herself in her office for days at a time, seemingly meeting with no one.

It was a hired spy that carried out this task. A message was pinned to Philetaerus's pillow by a jeweled dagger after the servants had prepared his rooms. It carried a simple request urging him to change his allegiance, with the promise of riches and position if he should do so while hinting he'd face certain death if he did not. The message was signed with the Vergina Sun of Macedonia.

She had to rely on the fact that if and when he chose to

approach someone to offer his support, that person would be smart enough to accept and offer him suitable rewards.

She tried to act surprised when news reached the court that he had joined Lysimachus. He had been rewarded richly indeed with a guardianship over a wealthy fortress and a substantial increase in status.

Cassander sent her a pointed stare after the messenger finished relaying the news.

"Have you been meddling?" he asked as he embraced her that night.

She kissed his cheek. "Of course not. You told me I was to stay out of politics."

"When have you ever listened?" Even in the dark, she could see his grin.

They finally managed to push back Antigonus. His allies had turned against him and he found himself surrounded. No one liked to see another person get too powerful.

Power was fickle and as tempting as any goddess.

"You must allow men to see you are strong but that you also share power," she whispered to Phillip at night.

"Won't they take it from me?"

"No, because while you will still hold most of the power, you will hide it and not show your hand too quickly. It's like when you give your horses free rein. They think they are in control and powerful, but in reality, you still hold the reins in your hand and can pull them back at any time. Do you see?"

Phillip nodded and she kissed the top of his dark head. Only Antipater had inherited Cassander's reddish hair. Her eldest son was fifteen now and did not like to be seen sitting around by his mother, but he visited her rooms or she came to him and he listened as she told him stories and taught him about ruling. He was in awe of this wise mother of his. Phillip saw how respected she was by everyone—even his father. It was through her that he could claim to be a blood relative of Alexander the Great. The myths about the great king were bountiful and he loved hearing about them, dreaming of one day following in his footsteps.

The next day she was overseeing the last tiles being set on the brilliant mosaic she had commissioned from the great artist Gnosis. It had actually been Phillip who inspired her to think of the subject matter. The mosaic showed Alexander and Hephaestion hunting a stag.

Thessalonike mused that she saw Alexander's face now more than she had ever seen it in real life. He had always been this larger-than-life figure, but she had never gotten to know the man behind the god's façade.

Cassander was weary these days. He was attending public events without his usual vigor and she regarded him now, wondering if his days were numbered. She had a strong desire to tighten her hold on her sons every time he looked tired, complained of chest pains, or called for the doctor.

She surprised herself by her cool regard for him. They were far gone from their tumultuous beginnings when she had sworn he would be forgotten by history and that he was weak. But she never cared for him like she had cared for the first love in her life.

She found herself thinking often of Maro lately. Remembering how they escaped the hot city in the summer and traveled to the more temperate coastal cities or the mountains with their cooling springs.

Sometimes he would appear to her in dreams. She would be young again and they would race down the sandy beach together. The waves would come dangerously close to lapping her away, but Maro kept her steady.

She did not consult with anyone about the meanings of these dreams, but she feared that if he was visiting her now it was an ominous sign her own death was near.

That summer she dubbed the summer of love. Ptolemy and Lysimachus married brides from each other's households. In total, there were three grand marriages that season and three gifts to be sent along with congratulations.

"Perhaps Phillip should be betrothed to someone—maybe Ptolemy's younger daughter?" she suggested to Cassander one night as they sat listening to a flute player.

"Not now, woman." He waved her away, and she ground her teeth to keep from lashing out at him.

She let the matter rest, but in her head she was calculating the days left until her son's coronation. Then she could arrange an appropriate match without Cassander's suffocating presence.

She felt more powerful than she had ever been before. She did not even mind the new aches and pains that came with age or that she had lost her smooth face and pretty looks. That was empty—she had tasted power and now she wanted more. If she could change things from the shadows, she would. She wanted respect. She wanted control. These things had always been sparing in her life.

Aigai, 297 BC

The cries of the mourners echoed in her head so loudly she could barely hear her own thoughts.

Today they would carry Cassander's body to his final resting place.

He had wished to be buried in the tombs of his ancestors. Taking his place among the white vaulted walls decorated with brilliant images of garlands and flowers, while the mosaics on the floor paid homage to the brilliant rich history of his family. The procession set out before dawn.

Walking behind her was Polyperchon's son, another Alexander. He was here to vote on the council tomorrow to reaffirm her son to his throne. When he had pledged his loyalty to her, she had been amused by his promises, but she trusted his sense of duty. Like his father before him, he valued honor and prestige above all else. The fact that she had it in her power to offer him generalship made her feel more secure.

All she would have to do was whisper in Phillips's ear and he would see her wishes were fulfilled. He was so unlike his father.

She felt nothing for the man who she had shared eighteen years of her life with. She had gone from hating him to accepting him to admiring him. Now there was nothing. In his last days, she had tended to him and tolerated him, but she had not adored him as a truly loving wife should.

She had not been able to make herself love the man who had ordered the deaths of her mother and nephew. As hypocritical as that was, for she had loved Olympias, who had commanded the deaths of countless loved ones and innocents alike. It had taken her a long time to realize that everyone had blood on their hands, even if they hadn't been the ones to yield the knife. No one was innocent.

Perhaps that was why the gods punished them so harshly.

It seemed to her that humanity was a doomed race. With bloodstained hands they conquered, they loved, and they fell.

She shook her head, clearing her mind of such dark brooding thoughts. No one seemed to notice she had not been paying attention to the lamentations made by the priests. In her thoughts she was safe.

Her two youngest sons walked in front of her. She imagined after their brother's coronation they would be found positions and she dared hope kingdoms for them as well. She regarded Antipater with a frown as he tried to nudge his younger brother with his foot as though trying to trip him up.

She quickened her pace and grabbed his arm, pulling him back roughly. He pierced her with a gaze so fierce she nearly let him go.

"Behave yourself. You can walk by my side," she commanded, not wishing to give way to her most difficult of sons.

"Alexander's the one bawling like a baby. The tears streaming down his cheeks as though he were a girl." Antipater sneered. "It's his fault if he is not paying attention and falls into the dirt."

"Be silent."

He looked at her coolly before looking chastised and giving her some half-hearted apology.

Alexander resembled her more than any of her children in temperament. He was more sensitive, but he was also wiser than his elder brothers. He was always studying, trying to cram as much knowledge as he could into his brain each night before falling asleep. He was not that skilled in combat, but he was a great archer and knew his way around a horse.

Of all her children, he had also been the closest to Cassander, though his father had barely tolerated him. She knew how much he looked up to him, and though she wished he would have picked a better role model, she did not discourage him. The loss of his father had affected him deeply.

Her attention turned to her eldest son—he was walking up ahead, standing tall. She could imagine his face set in a grim serious expression. He was only seventeen and would be asked to take up a huge responsibility running the kingdom, but she knew he would grow into it. He had plenty of advisors by his side, including her.

The procession reached the entrance of the tomb and Thessalonike's pondering ended. She stepped forward to take her place—she was the official mourner responsible for carrying out all the necessary rites.

She pulled a newly sharpened knife from her side and sliced into her right palm, deeper than was perhaps necessary. Letting the blood pool in the ceremonial bowl, she added a lock of her hair and the rest of the libations of honey and milk before she began reciting the prayer. All customs had to be observed.

Next came the offerings to the dead, more prayers, and then at last the cleansing would begin.

Her heart soared with anticipation.

AFTERWORD

To this day, Alexander the Great remains a prominent historical figure. He has far outshone his relatives and family to the point that they have nearly become invisible in popular culture.

I had the pleasure of coming across Thessalonike and was drawn in by her tragic story. She was his longest-surviving sibling in the ensuing battles after his death. Both Cynane and Cleopatra failed in their quests for power and glory but led equally exciting lives.

Thessalonike died only two years after Cassander's death. Her son Antipater had her executed for the favoritism she showed to her youngest son. Unfortunately, Phillip did not live long after his father's death, dying from disease a year later. This is when Thessalonike demanded that her remaining sons rule jointly.

This did not end well and Antipater drove Alexander

out of Macedonia, only to be later killed by Demetrius, who took control of Macedonia, thus ending Cassander's line.

There is little known about Thessalonike's movements and relationships. We do know she was raised by Olympias. Otherwise, she might have fallen into obscurity as the daughter of a lesser wife or been killed following Phillip's death. We also know she was with Olympias at Pydna when the fortress was besieged by Cassander, who later had Olympias executed and then married Thessalonike, with whom he had three children. The date of her actual birth is debated, but for this story I used 348 BC. Additionally, while I drew on real people living at the time, many of the events between 336-323 BC are fictional. It is plausible that she may have had betrothals before her eventual marriage to Cassander. However, the ones I mention in this book are fictional, as is her relationship with Maro. There is a myth that persists that after Alexander the Great's death she threw herself into the sea but instead of dying turned into a mermaid that haunted sailors. I incorporated that into this story.

I hope you have enjoyed reading this story.

Further Reading
Free short stories about Cynane and Cleopatra can be found at **www.annerbailey.com.**

Printed in Great Britain
by Amazon